for Marshall

HAVE YOU SEEN?

Griffin Gateaux

6'3"

205 pounds

Black Italian Suit

Black Coat

Black Shoes

Very Handsome

Brown Hair ~~not his own~~ [Gus wrote that]

~~Ego the size of North America~~ [more Gus]

~~Noticeable belly~~ [What belly? Gus is jealous!]

Anyone with information,
please contact
the Jenkins Detective Agency
317-555-2417

One

The day after Thanksgiving, my sister, Sam, lounged in the living room reading *The Economist* while I devoured three slices of leftover pie and obsessed over when Colin would call me. Colin was my closest friend in Venice; we'd kissed the night before and hadn't spoken since. I had spent the afternoon picking up the phone and checking that it still worked, and rehashing our final words from the previous night.

"He said, 'Sophie. See you,'" I told Sam. "Did he mean *See* you? See *YOU*? Or *Seeya*, as in *Seeya, that kiss sucked!*" I gave her a play-by-play of the kiss for the fifth time.

"I think he meant 'See you,' or maybe he meant YOU'RE DRIVING YOUR SISTER INSANE," she said, riffling the pages of her magazine.

I called my friend Mackenzie in hopes of getting a more helpful analysis.

"I'm sure he meant *See you as soon as possible,*" she said.

"Really? You think? It was so crowded in the diner last night, we didn't get to talk or anything after the kiss." Colin and I had kissed in the basement of the Petal Diner after the power went out during Turkeyluck, the diner's annual Thanksgiving potluck supper. It was the first time I'd ever kissed someone I really, really liked.

"You need to stop worrying," Mackenzie said.

"But why hasn't he called?" I asked.

"He's probably trying to call right now."

"You're right. I better get off the phone." We didn't have Call Waiting, since Sam thought it was a waste of money. I resumed my vigil staring at the receiver and munched on some turkey-shaped cookies; Wilda, the Petal Diner's owner, had sent Sam and me home with a huge platter of leftovers. While I ate, I picked up *Glamour* and checked if my horoscope gave any clue to the meaning of *See you*.

A little while later, I heard a strange noise outside. It sounded like the clopping of hooves.

"Did you hear that?" I asked Sam.

"Mmm, it means 'See you soon,'" she mumbled, not listening.

I peeked out the window. A horse and carriage was parked in front of our house, under the streetlight; Chester, our town mechanic, sat in the driver's seat.

Through the window I watched Colin step out of the buggy and head toward our front steps. I glanced at the mirror beside the door. I hadn't brushed my hair, I had a big orange splotch of dried Clearasil on my face, and I was wearing my rattiest sweatpants.

"*Get the door!*" I screamed at Sam. "I need to hide!"

"Huh?" She wrinkled her nose as the bell rang.

"*Get the door!*" I ran upstairs.

I listened from the hall and heard Zayde, our asthmatic cat, greet Colin with a loud fit of coughing.

"Is Sophie home?" Colin asked Sam.

"Yeah, sure...uh, just a sec."

Sam bounded upstairs. I waved her into the bathroom, where I'd begun to wash my face frantically.

"I can't believe Colin brought the carriage—apparently he's taking pointers from Josh," she said. Josh was
Sam's boyfriend; he'd taken her for a ride in Chester's
carriage a couple weeks before. "You better hurry up,
he's waiting."

"I can't go down there like this! I look hideous," I
said. "Oh my God. What am I going to wear?"

"Soph. It's Colin. He doesn't care what you're wearing. He sees you practically every day."

"This is different. This is postkiss. I have to look post-
kiss-worthy."

She sighed.

"Just stall him," I said, waving her toward the stairs.
"I'm hurrying."

I moisturized, brushed my hair, undressed, tried on
three different outfits, and finally picked a pair of jeans
and a red sweater. I quickly applied mascara and lip
gloss and a spritz of perfume.

When I came downstairs Zayde was sprawled on
Colin's lap, happily snoring, and Sam was discussing
taxes with Colin.

"Most business equipment has to be depreciated
over either five or seven years, so you'd have a first-year
deduction of only twenty percent of the cost of five-year
property."

Colin was doing a good job of pretending to look interested. He grinned when he saw me.

"Sorry if I caught you at a bad time," he said. "I tried calling earlier but it was busy, so I thought I'd just surprise you."

"It's not a bad time."

"I thought maybe we could go to the movies," he said.

"Sure! Sounds great!" My voice squeaked like an overeager cheerleader's.

"What movie are you going to see?" Sam asked.

"Well—it's a surprise." Colin smiled. "It's at a new movie theater in town—the Venice Theatre."

"I haven't heard anything about a new theater," Sam said.

"I don't think that many people know about it yet. Tonight's the premiere showing," he said, and raised an eyebrow.

Sam squinted. "What's the movie rated?"

"I don't know. Probably G, I think."

"G. I guess that's okay." She nodded. "Well, be back by ten. No dillydallying." I rolled my eyes at Sam's last comment. But I guess I couldn't fault her for trying. Sam was my legal guardian, if you applied a broad definition to the word *legal*. Our parents had both died, our mom six years ago and our dad last summer, leaving our creepy, diet-addicted stepmother, Enid Gutmyre, to inherit everything. Enid had wanted to separate Sam and me by shipping me off to a boarding school in Canada. To prevent that from happening, Sam transferred our dad's money into an account of our own, we fled New

York City, and ended up here in Venice, Indiana, under the new names of Sam and Fiona Scott. (I got stuck with the embarrassing new name, though I told people to call me Sophie.) No one in Venice knew who we really were—not even Colin.

He and I said good-bye to Sam and walked out the door.

"Sophie, come here a sec," Sam called after me.

"What?" I asked. I went back inside while Colin waited on the porch.

"Be careful," Sam whispered.

"Isn't the buggy safe? You rode in it."

"Yeah, it's safe. Just, uh—you'll be back by ten? Promise?" she asked.

"Sure." I had no idea what she was so worried about. I hugged her good-bye and walked with Colin to the carriage.

"Onward?" Chester asked Colin, and winked at me.

"Onward," Colin said.

Colin helped me get settled in the buggy and placed a wool blanket over my lap. His dark brown bangs fell into his eyes, and when he smiled my throat dried up. I tried to act normally, like I had before the kiss, but the kiss was like another entity between us. I could barely remember how I'd ever been casual with him before. Suddenly everything had changed.

"I had a lot of fun at the Turkeyluck," I said.

"Me, too," he said.

I tried to think of something else to say, but I didn't need to because Chester started chatting up a storm.

"Many people don't know this, but what doomed the horse and carriage wasn't just the automobile, but another invention you know quite well—yep, the bicycle. Between 1889 and 1899 the production of bicycles in this country went from two hundred thousand to one million, believe it or not. In 1866, Richard Dudgeon built a steam-powered carriage, which led to a steam-powered bicycle—and then the motorcycle was not far behind that..."

I might have found this lecture interesting if it wasn't for the fact that I wanted to be kissing Colin again. As Chester continued on about the rise of the automobile, I couldn't stop thinking about what might happen between Colin and me.

I thought back to all the guys I'd had huge crushes on before (not counting the embarrassing ones on various boy-band members). I realized my entire romantic life could be summed up on the fingers of one hand:

1. *Randy Chaefsky, NYC, February 2003.* Somewhat skeezy artist dude from LaGuardia High School of the Arts, my old school. One random makeout session on empty subway train. Slobbery kisser.

2. *Troy Howard, Venice, August 2003.* Lifeguard with incredible chest muscles. Major lack of brain cells. Colossal fidelity issues. One bad date to the Slow Down Hoe Down restaurant. Owns a cute dog, though.

3. *Pete Teagarden, Venice, September 2003.*
Mechanics classmate, aspiring NFL player/chef
with octopus tendencies; proclivity toward
General Tso's chicken, which he thinks is
pronounced as General Teeso's. One bad date to
Chinese restaurant.

4. *Jack Jenkins, Las Vegas, November 2003.* Tall,
dark, talented, and my boss Gus's son. One
extremely embarrassing failed attempt to kiss
him; would prefer to permanently erase it from
my memory. Turned out to be gay.

5. *Colin Wright, Thanksgiving 2003.* Chocolate
brown hair, soulful brown eyes, lopsided smile.
Out-of-this-world kiss.

Colin touched my hand; Chester had stopped talking.
"What are you thinking about?" Colin asked.
"Oh nothing." I was thinking: Would number five be
the real thing?

Chester stopped the horse and carriage in front of a
brick house.
"The Venice Theatre," Chester announced. "Mi'lady,
mi'lord, I hope you enjoy yourselves."
Mi'lady? Had Chester been hanging out at
Renaissance festivals? He tied up the horse and then
joined us on the sidewalk.
"Why are we at Fred's house?" I asked.
"Fred's been working on turning their old barn into a
little projection theater," Colin said.

The three of us walked into the backyard. A sign on the barn said:

WELCOME TO THE VENICE THEATRE!
VENICE'S ONLY ART HOUSE CINEMA

TONIGHT'S SHOWING:
CLARK GABLE and
CLAUDETTE COLBERT in
IT HAPPENED ONE NIGHT

"I found the projector at a yard sale and I gave it to Fred a few months ago," Colin said. "He's finally got it working."

We ran into Mackenzie inside the barn. She gave me a big hug.

"Why didn't you tell me about this?" I asked.

"Fred wanted it to be hush-hush," she said. "I think he's afraid the sound's not going to work or something. He doesn't want to humiliate himself in front of everyone, so he told me not to say anything."

I looked around the barn. A screen hung from one wall, rows of folding chairs had been set up, and a space heater was going full blast. Fred was fiddling with the projector in back. His entire family was sitting in the front row, including his aunt Erma and uncle Bernie. Herman, Fred's elderly Labrador retriever, occupied a prime spot right next to the space heater, and was fast asleep.

Fred moved in front of the screen and cleared his throat. "I'm here to welcome you to the first ever film showing at the Venice Theatre...we have refreshments to offer—thanks, Aunt Erma"—she started passing around bags of popcorn and cans of Coke— "and we're proud to present tonight's feature, which is one of the greatest romantic comedies of all time. It was directed by Frank Capra, and it won the top five Academy Awards in 1934—"

"Start the movie!" Bernie shouted.

"Okay, okay. Relax, sit back, and enjoy the show. And, uh, please turn off your cell phones." No one made a move—cell phones had yet to become ubiquitous in Venice.

"Thanks." Fred smiled and disappeared behind the projector.

I'd seen *It Happened One Night* before and I loved it, but I found it hard to pay attention during the movie. It was dark in Fred's barn, and I kept peeking over at Colin. I hoped he might reach for my hand or do something, but he seemed intent on watching the film. I guessed it wasn't the most private, romantic situation anyway; Erma kept sneezing and coughing and Bernie liked to shout advice to the actors on screen. "Run faster, son! Faster!" he yelled at Clark Gable as Clark chased a man who'd stolen Claudette Colbert's suitcase.

"Someone needs to tell him Clark's not gonna hear him," I whispered to Colin.

He nodded. "I know." He kept staring at the screen.

As I watched Clark and Claudette nearly kiss as they

spent the night in a hay field, I thought of when I first saw Colin in his store, Wright Bicycles, Etc. I'd had a feeling from everything in his shop—shelves and shelves of used novels and poetry, quirky tchotchkes, and lovingly restored bikes—that Colin and I would be friends. I loved that he cared so much about these lost, forgotten things, that he fixed them and found them new homes. So why was it so scary to fall for such a good friend?

Because I didn't want to get my heart broken.

That was it. To turn it into something more was like jumping off a cliff. I could so easily go *splat* at the bottom.

The movie neared its end. "Amen," Bernie shouted when Clark and Claudette finally got together.

After the last scene, Erma passed around more popcorn and a bowl of homemade rock candy. Colin helped Fred with the projector and Mackenzie and I moved to a corner.

"So what's going on with you and Colin?" she whispered.

"I might be able to tell you if we could actually get a second alone together." I told her about Chester's lecture on horse-and-carriage history.

"Maybe Chester will leave you alone on the way back. A carriage is really romantic." She nodded.

"I know." I smiled.

Chester did keep quiet for the first part of the ride home, but Colin seemed oddly silent, too. I hoped he was just nervous—I certainly was; I felt like my heart was about to pound its way through my chest. But I wanted him to make the first move.

I tilted my head back, closed my eyes, and loosened my lips, trying to look utterly kissable. After a few seconds in this position I opened one eye and snuck a peek at him.

"Are you okay?" Colin asked. "You look like you're falling asleep."

I sat up and smoothed the blanket over my legs. "No—I'm, uh, fine."

I sighed. As we trotted past Main Street, Chester decided to pipe in: "That movie just gets me every time. They don't make 'em like that anymore. Why not? I wonder. What happened to simple old-fashioned falling in love? Now they got—*computer animation*," he drawled, as if it was a disease, "and *special effects*. What does it get you? Nothing. Just—just gimme a good love story, that's all I ask."

I'd give you some old-fashioned romance if you'd please stop talking, I wanted to say.

A minute later, we'd reached my house.

"Want me to wait, Col—I mean, gentleman, sir?" Chester asked.

"Thanks, but that's okay. I can walk home from here," Colin said.

"Thanks, Chester. It was really fun," I said.

"Thanks for the pushrods," Chester told Colin.

"Anytime," Colin said. As we walked up the steps of my porch, he explained, "Chester gave me the carriage ride in exchange for some car parts I got him for the '58 Ford he's rebuilding."

I paused on our porch. The windows of the houses

across the street were all dark. "I had a great time," I told him.

"So did I."

The porch light was off, and we stood in the cold, our breath billowing out like wispy clouds. Did he want to kiss me again? Or was he having second thoughts? There could be a long-winded we-should-just-be-friends speech any minute. But then why get the carriage? To let me down easy?

He stepped toward me. The porch light flashed on and the door swung open.

"There you are!" Sam shouted, as if she'd been looking for us for days.

"We'll be inside in a minute," I told her.

"It's ten-fifteen."

"So?" I asked.

"You said you'd be home by ten."

"What's the difference?"

"I was worried."

"For fifteen minutes?"

She folded her arms. "It's freezing out. Why don't you come inside?"

I sent her a long pleading look but she stood there waiting, hopping from foot to foot.

Colin said, "I should be getting home anyway." He patted me on the back—*a pat on the back! Not even a hug!*—and before I could figure out what to say, he walked down the steps and disappeared around the corner.

Two

"Why did you do that?" I asked Sam as I stomped into the living room.

"Do what?"

"Ruin my date? Why couldn't you leave us alone?" I sat down on the couch and placed my head in my hands.

"You were alone in the buggy."

"No, we were with Chester, who talked the whole time."

She bit her lip. "Oh. Did he tell you the whole history of the horse-drawn carriage? That's what he did when Josh and I rode with him."

"As a matter of fact he did. So why did you interrupt us?"

She sighed and sat down beside me. "Soph. I think we need to discuss something."

I gazed at her. "What?"

She took a deep breath. "When a girl gets to be a certain age—fifteen, say, like you—things happen. And when a boy reaches that age—other things happen."

Oh no. She wasn't saying this.

"Boys Colin's age…well, they're, shall we say, preoccupied. They don't really think about what they're doing—at least they don't think with their brains, ha ha ha," she said.

I tried not to laugh. My sister, who'd had a total of about half a dozen dates in her life, was giving me a birds-and-the-bees talk? Did she think I was eight years old? I had actually absorbed some information, if not from my own experience per se, then from movies, books, magazines, the Internet, and simply existing in the world. But for the fun of it, I pretended I had no idea where this was going.

"What do you mean?" I asked innocently.

She sighed again. "I know Colin's a good guy. I just— I want to watch out for you. I hope you two will take your time with things."

"Things?"

"You know—stuff," she said.

"Stuff?"

She scrunched her eyes and I finally said, "Don't worry. It's Colin—you know he's trustworthy. You didn't worry when I went out with Troy or Pete."

"That was different, though—I knew you'd never be serious about them."

I cheered a little at that—she thought Colin and I had the potential to be serious?

"I'll be fine. All we've done so far is that one kiss. You don't need to worry," I said.

"I do worry. It's my job. I don't know how Mommy and Daddy did it, looking out for us all the time." She shook her head. I really did feel bad for her sometimes, that she felt like a parent even though she was just two years older than me. It couldn't be that easy, being the official guardian.

"So what did you do all night?" I asked her, trying to change the subject.

"Not much—I can't wait for Josh to get back tomorrow. I read, watched *Wall Street Week* and *Inside Indiana Business*. Oh—Wilda called and left a message for you. She wants your 'brioche' recipe."

"Uh-oh."

"Just don't slip and call it challah." For the Turkeyluck potluck dinner I'd shown Colin how to make challah bread—the traditional Jewish bread that's eaten on the Sabbath—though I hadn't called it challah, I'd called it brioche. This was because along with not knowing we were actually Samantha and Sophia Shattenberg of Sunnyside, Queens, neither Colin, nor anyone else in Venice, had any idea that Sam and I were Jewish. As far as they knew, we were Christian, from Cleveland, and arrived in Venice after a car accident killed our parents. That was our official story—we couldn't tell anyone who we were, since our stepmother, Enid, and the detective she'd hired, Hal Hertznick, might still be trying to track us down.

"So tell me about your date," Sam said.

I sighed. "You don't need to worry about Colin. I don't know if anything more is going to happen with us. It was just one kiss." I sank deeper into the couch. "That's it."

She looked relieved.

I didn't tell her how much I was secretly hoping that our relationship would turn out to be a lot more than just one kiss.

I stopped by the Petal Diner Saturday morning to give Wilda the recipe. The diner was still recovering from the Turkeyluck; the counter was cluttered with the remains of four different pies, and Wilda's cat, Betty, was gleefully guarding a huge pile of turkey scraps in her food dish. It was early and I was the only customer.

Wilda bustled around, cleaning up. She gave me coffee and a cinnamon roll. "I just *lovvved* those brioche rolls you and Colin made. I can't stop thinking about them. I've made brioche before, but yours was sweeter, and a little denser, I think. They had more substance, but they weren't too heavy. Delicious!"

"It was my mom's recipe," I said. I took out the index card that I'd written the recipe on and handed it to her. It had been easy to disguise the challah recipe as brioche, since the two were pretty similar.

"Your mom must have been a fabulous chef."

"She was." I sighed. I missed her so much sometimes. It still amazed me that she could be gone for so many years—I still thought of her all the time. Just the other night I'd dreamed of her, that she was still alive and living in Indiana and we didn't even know it. Indianapolis was where she'd disappeared—she'd been the victim of a carjacking, and it wasn't until two years after her disappearance that she was declared dead, after DNA evidence was found linking a man to the crime.

I took a deep breath. It was so much easier to try to block it out of my mind. Sometimes I couldn't believe that what had happened to our parents had actually taken place. I felt like it must have happened to someone else, that such horrible things couldn't strike *us*. I had to stop my mind from going down that road. *Remember the good things*, our dad used to tell us about our mom. Her voice, her love of music and art, how it felt when she hugged us, the foods she cooked.

"She was a great cook," I said. I took a bite of the cinnamon roll. "She made the best ma—" I was about to say matzo-ball soup, but stopped myself.

"I'm sure she was the best ma ever," Wilda said, nodding sadly.

"She was. And she also made the best soup. We used to make it together."

"What kind?" Wilda asked.

"It was, uh—dumpling soup," I said.

"Flour dumplings? Potato?"

"Um, uh, cracker meal, actually," I said. That's what matzo balls were, really—ground-up crackers.

"Cracker meal?" Wilda placed her hand on her hip. "I never heard of a cracker dumpling before."

"They're so good. Mmmm." I smiled, remembering.

"Can you give me the cracker dumpling recipe, too?"

"Uh…I don't think we have it written down," I said. "My mom sort of just made things up." I smiled, trying to sound like I was telling the truth, regretting ever having mentioned it.

"Well, do you remember it at all? Maybe you can just write down what you remember. I'm curious—I never had a cracker dumpling before!"

She gave me a pink index card and a pen. I paused. How would I invent a fake matzo ball?

She watched me. "Do you want to come into the kitchen? That always helps me—once I see all the ingredients in front of me and start to cook, it all comes back. You can just give me a general idea of what goes in it. You know I'm always looking for new ideas...I was actually making some soup for lunch with the leftover turkey scraps—it's simmering in there. Come on, bring your cinnamon roll."

Before I knew it, she had picked up my coffee cup and was leading me into the kitchen. I did feel kind of honored to be back there, since she seldom let people actually enter her sacred kitchen.

I decided I'd just wing it and make up a recipe as I went along, and hopefully she wouldn't figure it out. After all, there had to be other cracker meal dumplings in the universe, right? At least I hoped there were.

She put on an apron that was silk-screened with humongous multicolored cat faces. She smiled, looking excited.

"Okay...first you, um, just take any crackers you have on hand," I said.

Wilda pulled out a box of Ritz and I tried not to cringe. Ritz crackers were a far cry from matzo.

"Then you grind them up with a mortar and pestle." I was lying my head off—the first step in our recipe was to buy the ground matzo meal at the grocery store.

Wilda took out a mortar and pestle and started grinding the crackers; I glanced at the little TV on the kitchen shelf. The food station was on. On the screen, a really good-looking man in a suit was dipping bread into different olive oils. "C'est magnifique! *In this oil I can taste notes of sage and myrtle. Lovely. Many chefs don't realize that olive oil can be substituted for other fats in a slew of recipes, and it's very healthy. I once heard of a woman in Provence who drank an ounce of olive oil every day and lived to be a hundred and twenty-six!*"

The camera cut to a field of sunflowers, and an old woman walking by in a huge floppy hat.

Wilda stared at the set. "*Griffin on the Go,*" she said. "I love that show."

"A hundred and twenty-six?" I asked. "From drinking olive oil?"

She shrugged. "He's always full of stories and tips—he'll eat anything. He once did a show in Japan and ate blowfish, which can kill you. People die every year from it. He goes to different towns all over the world; he's hardly ever in America." She finished grinding the crackers. "Next step?"

I told her to add beaten eggs. "Then you add the schm...alt," I stammered. I was thinking of *schmaltz,* which is the Yiddish word for "chicken fat," but I couldn't say that.

"Shmalt?" Wilda asked.

"I mean the salt," I said. I breathed deeply. "Just a pinch should be fine. And then add the fat...a few tablespoons of oil to the batter...maybe olive oil," I added cheerfully.

She nodded, added the salt and oil, and mixed the batter.

"That's it," I said. "You shape them into little

dumplings, boil them, then add them to the soup. It's good to boil them separately so that they don't get bits of starch in the stock."

I tried to think of something else to make them less matzo-ball-ish. "Oh, and I almost forgot, you have to add"—my eyes scanned the spice racks on the shelves—"sesame seeds."

Wilda nodded, and dutifully added sesame seeds. Then she shaped the batter into balls and dropped them into a pot of boiling water. We watched them rise to the surface. To my relief they looked nothing like matzo balls; they were tiny and sort of a caramel color.

After they'd simmered for twenty minutes, we added them to the turkey broth, and tasted it.

Wilda closed her eyes as she chewed a dumpling. "I like it. Is this how it's supposed to taste?"

They tasted like rubbery sesame Ritz crackers. "Sort of. Although maybe my mom added something else that I'm leaving out." *Such as matzo*. I shrugged.

The bells at the front door jingled; we poked our heads into the diner and watched Gus Jenkins walk in. Sam worked for Gus full-time at the Jenkins Detective Agency, which specialized in finding missing persons, and I helped out after school and on weekends. We'd already helped solve three cases since we'd come to Venice. The last one had involved tracking down Gus's estranged son, Jack, who was romantic interest number four on my list—before I learned that he was gay, that is.

"You're up early," Wilda said to Gus. "Here for breakfast?"

He nodded. "My stomach was growling all night. The more you stuff yourself on Thanksgiving, the hungrier you are for days afterward—ever notice that?"

"Well, don't get too hungry—you've been looking very svelte lately," Wilda told him.

It was true: Gus was looking really good; he'd lost a lot of weight since Sam and I'd first met him, and was doing so much better overall. The first time we saw Gus's office it looked like a garbage dump, with piles of papers, beer cans, and junk everywhere; you couldn't even see the floor. Now, with Sam's help, the wood floors gleamed and the place was almost spotless.

"Thank you," Gus said. "I feel pretty good. You look nice yourself," he said to Wilda.

I did a double take; Gus wasn't one for handing out compliments, and he didn't even comment on the eight huge cat faces smiling at him from Wilda's apron. Reconciling with his son must have had a huge impact on him. Jack had surprised Gus at the Turkeyluck; he only stayed in town for two nights, but it seemed like he and Gus had made some huge steps toward smoothing out their differences.

Gus sat down at the counter. Wilda brought him a mug of coffee and a bowl of our soup.

"This is breakfast? What the hell's floating in that?" Gus asked, staring at the ground-up Ritz cracker balls.

"It's for lunch, but I want you to taste it. It's dumpling soup," Wilda said. "It's delicious. It's Sophie's mom's recipe."

"Sort of her recipe—" I said. My stomach clenched;

would he recognize its resemblance to matzo-ball soup?

Gus looked skeptical as he stared at the brown balls bobbing around. "They look like doughnut holes." He tried one. "Interesting," he said.

He slurped the soup and bit into another Ritz ball. "It's really not too bad," he said, surprised. He finished the whole bowl and then ate a cinnamon roll, too.

"I'm glad you like it," Wilda said sweetly.

Gus glanced at her. "Cute apron."

I blinked. Did Gus actually just say "cute apron"?

"Sophie, do you mind checking on the soup pot? I left it on simmer but I think you should turn it down more and stir it a little."

"Okay," I said, and wandered into the kitchen.

At the counter, Wilda lowered her voice and asked Gus, "Did you hear about the new theater that Fred Lamb started?"

"No, I didn't," Gus said.

"Chester told me about it."

She said something else that I couldn't hear; I moved closer to the door to listen.

"Never heard of it," Gus was saying.

"It's a great movie. I'd love to go see it sometime. I bet you'd like it, too." She refilled his coffee mug. "You're...you looked very handsome at Turkeyluck."

My mouth fell open: Wilda was unabashedly flirting with Gus! They'd been friends for a long time, and in October we'd convinced Wilda to ask Gus to the Sadie Hawkins dance; they'd seemed to have a good time together, but I hadn't noticed anything happening between them since.

I tried to send Gus a mental message: *Just ask her to the movies!*

But he didn't. He seemed completely clueless about what she was hinting at. Gus probably wouldn't notice a woman was interested in him even if you bonked him on the head with her.

Finally, Wilda gave up hinting.

"Do you want to go with me?" she asked him.

He slurped his coffee noisily.

"Sure," he said. "Why not?"

Gus, you're the epitome of romance, I whispered.

When I got home I told Sam, "Wilda just asked Gus on a date! You should've seen it—they were *flirting*."

"How does Gus flirt?" Sam asked. "'*You're a nice broad,*'" she said in a fake-Gus voice.

I laughed, and described their whole conversation.

"I can't believe he said 'why not?'" Sam shook her head. "We need to send him to charm school. So did you give Wilda the *brioche* recipe?"

"I, uh—I did." I smiled nervously.

She squinted at me. "What? What's the problem? Did she figure out that it's challah?" Her face started turning pink.

"No—no." I flopped down onto the couch. "It's just that brioche and sesame Ritz-cracker-ball soup might soon be on the Petal Diner menu." I explained what had happened with Wilda. "But believe me, those 'dumplings' had no resemblance to a matzo ball whatsoever."

"Are you sure?"

"They tasted like eggy glueballs and they were

brown and small and weird. Don't worry—I mean, have you ever tasted a sesame-flavored matzo ball made out of Ritz crackers?"

She shook her head. "Good point. It sounds disgusting. But in the future, let's not let any comments about latkes or hamantaschen slip out, okay?"

"Okay." I peered at the phone. "Did, um, anyone call for me?"

"No, Colin didn't call for you," she said.

"I wasn't asking about him," I said, though of course I was. I'd hoped he would call while I was out. "Is Josh back yet?"

"He's supposed to get back sometime today—soon I hope." Sam had met Josh while we were attempting to solve our second missing persons case—Josh's grandfather, Leo Shattenberg, had hired us to find Leo's old girlfriend. Because Shattenberg was our real last name, too, we'd thought that Leo and Josh might be our long lost relatives. It turned out that they weren't, which was good since Josh had a huge crush on my sister, and she liked him, too, though she understandably wasn't too keen on the idea of dating her cousin.

"He said he'd come over later, but I don't know what we're going to do tonight yet," Sam said. "Maybe I'll take him to Fred's new movie thing. What are you up to? Are you going to see Colin again?"

"I hope so."

She looked anxious all of a sudden. "I, um, I got something for you this morning." She pulled a book out of her knapsack and gave it to me. "They had it at the library."

I stared at the pink cover. *How Babies Are Created*. "Didn't you used to have this book?" I asked. I was pretty sure I'd seen it in her room ages ago.

She nodded. "Daddy gave it to me when I was like ten. I left it in Queens, though."

I flipped through it. There were illustrations of chickens, dogs, and various farm animals mating.

"Yuck! These pigs are doing it." The final chapter featured humans doing the same thing, discreetly covered with a sheet. The book looked like it was about forty years old; I don't know where our dad had ever gotten it in the first place. I closed the cover. "Sam, I know all this. I'm not five years old, and I wasn't raised in a barn. Although apparently it wouldn't make a difference if I was."

She sat on her bed. "I know. I just…I don't know how to talk to you about all this stuff. I just want you to…just be careful, okay?"

"I'll try." I couldn't believe she was so worried. "But he hasn't even called. At this point I'd be happy if Colin remembered my name. Then again, I'd be overjoyed if he started attacking me and ripping all my clothes off."

She raised an eyebrow. "Overjoyed?"

"I'm kidding." I looked in the book again. "These chickens look really happy, though."

I decided to get proactive about the Colin situation— no more waiting for the phone to ring. I was going to call him. I spent the next hour inhaling deeply and practicing what I would casually say when I called—lots of versions of *Hi! What's up?* in about ten different tones.

When I finally worked up the courage to dial his number, he wasn't there. I listened to his voice on the answering machine, then hung up; I hadn't prepared what to say in a message. *Hi! What's up?* wasn't going to work.

I thought about just stopping by his place instead. I'd casually stopped by his store a hundred times before, but now I didn't know how to do it without feeling like a troupe of gymnasts were somersaulting in my stomach.

I spent the next hour perfecting my hair and doing my makeup to look like I had no makeup on at all, and then I casually strolled over to his shop, a few blocks away.

It was locked and the front door had the "Closed" sign up.

I sighed, gave up, went home, and read *I Capture the Castle,* my new favorite book, until I fell asleep on our couch. I woke up to a loud knock on the door.

Sam stood at the top of the stairs. "Who is it?" she called to me.

I opened the door and stared into the branches of a huge evergreen tree.

"It's not a who, it's a tree," I yelled to Sam.

"Soph," the tree said. "It's me. I'm back here." Through the branches I caught a glimpse of Colin's hat.

"Here—can you help me? Can you grab that end?" he asked.

I took the end of the tree and he managed to smush it through the door and into our living room.

"I was at the tree farm today, so I got two," he said. "I noticed you hadn't gotten yours yet."

"Thanks!" I said. I was so happy to see him; I smiled

goofily, unsure of what else to say. Did a tree count as a romantic gesture? Like flowers, only bigger?

He leaned the tree against one wall, stepped back, and brushed off his hands as Sam came bounding down the stairs.

She paused. "Hey…wow…nice tree."

"Colin got it for us at the tree farm," I said.

"Thanks," she told him. "But, um, isn't it kind of early for a Christmas tree?"

"Everyone in Venice gets their trees over Thanksgiving weekend," Colin said matter-of-factly. "Where are your ornaments?"

"Oh. We have them around somewhere," I lied. "I wonder where we put them?" I asked Sam.

She bit her lip. "I don't think I packed them when we left Cleveland…they made me too sad, I guess, or something—the memories." She shrugged and stared down at the floor. It was an Oscar-worthy performance.

Colin nodded. "I can understand that." He was probably thinking of his mother, who had died of breast cancer three years ago. He picked pine needles off of his jacket. "Do you want some new ones? I've got a bunch of ornaments in the shop—I haven't even looked through them yet."

"Are you sure? Don't you want to sell those?" I asked.

He shook his head. "I have tons. I'll go get them." He headed for the door, and then paused. "Do you have a Christmas-tree stand?"

"Our old one broke—we threw it out last year," Sam said.

Colin said, "I've got an extra one, too—I'll go get it. Be back in a sec."

We watched him walk out the door. When he was gone, we both stared at the tree.

"I hope he believed us," Sam said.

"I can't believe these crazy Venice people get their trees two days after Thanksgiving." I shrugged. I'd never heard of anyone doing that before.

Sam shook her head. "*I* can't believe we have a Christmas tree." She looked up at the ceiling. "Sorry, Dad!"

I stared at the ceiling and said "Sorry," too, as if our dad's spirit was just hanging out up there, floating around. When I was a kid, I'd always wanted to celebrate Christmas—it had always seemed like so much fun. We used to beg our parents to let us, but our father always said: *You're Jewish. And no, there's no such thing as a Chanukah bush.* Once, after we'd worn our dad down with our incessant pleading—I think it was the year after our mother disappeared, so he was feeling sad and easygoing—he let us put decorations all over the ficus in our living room. A bit pathetic, to say the least. The poor ficus had almost split in two under the weight of the ornaments. But now that we finally had a tree, I wasn't sure I wanted it. I'd have preferred to celebrate Chanukah like we did before.

Colin came back a few minutes later with a tree stand and a cardboard box. "I take no responsibility for what these ornaments look like—I got some of them from an estate sale in Indy, so who knows what's in here."

He set the tree up in the stand, and Zayde started

sniffing the pine needles. The phone rang and Sam answered it while I took the ornaments out of the box. Some were beautiful, including handblown glass bulbs and snowflakes, but after I unwrapped the top layer of ornaments, I looked down into the box. The eyes of about thirty miniature plush ferret ornaments stared back at me.

"Oh my God. These people had a serious ferret fetish."

There were ferrets skiing, ferrets golfing, ferrets skating, ferrets performing surgery, ferrets sunbathing, a Santa ferret, elf ferret, businessman ferret, and ferrets dressed as sheep and camels.

"This is kind of cute, in a horrifying way," I said. There were even ferret angels, with tiny furry ferret wings.

Colin laughed when he saw them. Zayde picked the golfing ferret up with her mouth and started batting it around the floor.

Sam got off the phone and came back into the living room. "Josh called—he's on his way over—he should be here any minute. What are *those*?"

"They're for the tree," I said, holding up a ferret in each hand.

"Perhaps there's a reason why these people gave their ornaments away," she said.

The doorbell rang a few minutes later, and Josh engulfed Sam in a huge hug. He gave Colin and me hugs also, and then glanced at the tree.

"Colin got it for us—isn't it nice?" Sam asked him.

She squeezed his hand, and I knew that squeeze had several meanings, since Josh was one of the three people in the Midwest who actually knew that we were Jewish, and what our real identities were. Josh's grandfather, Leo, and Tony Difriggio, our contact in the Midwestern underworld who'd helped us resettle in Indiana, were the other two people who knew.

We hadn't planned on Josh and Leo finding out, but Hertznick, the private detective our stepmother had hired, had tracked down Leo, thinking he might be our relative, too. Leo and Josh had stood up to Hertznick for us and lied for us, telling him that we weren't the girls he was looking for. Since then, we trusted Josh and Leo not to give our secret away.

"It's a great tree," Josh said. "Most guys just bring flowers!" He stared at the pile of ornaments beside it. "Nice weasels you have there, too."

"They're ferrets," Sam said.

Colin picked up the Santa ferret and laughed, then handed it to me. His fingers lingered on my hand.

Sam watched us.

"How about I take you out to dinner?" Josh asked my sister.

She looked toward Colin and then toward me and said, "What are you two doing for dinner?"

Colin and I exchanged glances. "Maybe we can stay here and order a pizza," he suggested.

I smiled. We'd finally get to be alone. "Sounds perfect."

"It does. Let's do that, too," Sam quickly told Josh. "I

think I might be coming down with a cold, so it would be nice to take it easy here, with Soph and Colin." She mustered a completely fake cough. "Plus I really want to decorate the tree together. We can string popcorn!" she said excitedly.

Josh shrugged and took off his coat. "Okay. Sounds fun."

I gave Sam a look. If it was up to her, Colin and I would never have a moment alone. I shouldn't have joked about the chickens in the book.

"I'll go make some hot chocolate," I said, trying not to sound forlorn.

"I'll help you." Sam followed me into the kitchen.

"It's okay to leave me and Colin alone—I wasn't serious when I said I wanted Colin to attack me," I whispered to her while I boiled the milk.

"I know," she said, though from her tone it didn't sound like she did. "I just thought it would be fun to stay here and string popcorn."

"What do you know about stringing popcorn?"

"Mrs. Murphy taught us how to do it in sixth grade," she said.

I took out a bag of marshmallows. "Hmmph."

She dusted off our popcorn maker and started popping. "I think we have some dried cranberries around somewhere, too. We can add them to the garland."

I brought the hot chocolate out to Josh and Colin, who were already putting the various ferrets on the tree. "Do you want these in any specific place?" Josh asked, holding the skier and ice-skater ferrets.

"Anywhere's fine," I said.

"Don't be too cavalier—we need to achieve an artistic ferret composition," Colin said.

"Oh, of course," I said, and smiled.

Sam brought out a huge bowl of popcorn. "Don't eat it all—we have to string half of it," she said while we kept hanging the ornaments.

I stood closely beside Colin. Our arms brushed each other and a chill traveled down my back.

"Too bad you don't have any mistletoe," Josh said with a wink.

Sam pinched him and mumbled something I couldn't hear. "It's just mistletoe," he mumbled to her.

Colin whispered to me, "I'll have to bring some next time."

I grinned. "Not as long as my sister's around," I whispered back.

Sam ordered the pizza, and I found a radio station that was playing nonstop holiday music. The four of us finished putting the ferrets on the tree—from a distance it looked like there were fuzzy brown socks hanging all over it—and then we sat down to string the popcorn and cranberries. Sam threaded four separate needles so we could each make part of the garland.

I tried to think of ways to sneak off alone for a minute with Colin. What could I say? That I had something important to discuss with him in the broom closet?

The doorbell rang; the pizza arrived. While Sam looked through her wallet to pay, I saw a furry blob run past the pizza boy and out the door.

Zayde!

I panicked—she'd run away once before and had gotten lost for almost a week—I ran out the door, and Colin followed behind me. We chased after Zayde as she raced around the house and under the neighbor's fence; she bounded through three different yards and disappeared around the corner. I let out a yelp and ran faster. I saw her shimmy under a neighbor's porch. I crouched down.

Zayde was having an asthma attack. She coughed and coughed, sounding like a cross between a seal and a barking dog. When she finally stopped coughing she slowly stepped out from under the porch. I lifted her up in my arms.

Before I could say anything, Colin swooped toward us and gathered me into a passionate kiss.

This was the second time Zayde had been sandwiched between us while we kissed—after she'd gotten lost, we'd found her in the basement of the Petal Diner on Thanksgiving.

Zayde was our Cupid. I loved that cat.

Three

By Sunday all traces of Thanksgiving decor had disappeared from Venice, and the town was swept into a true Christmas frenzy. Plastic snowmen appeared on top of every streetlight on Main Street, and glittery reindeer pranced alongside the dry canal bed that gave our town its name. Most of the homes downtown were transformed into twinkling gingerbread houses with sprawling Nativity scenes on their lawns. Even Fred decided to show *It's a Wonderful Life* nonstop at his new theater.

"I can't believe we're doing this," Sam said as we hung icicle lights above our porch on Sunday night.

"We need to blend in with the neighborhood," I said.

We went shopping at the It's Christmas! store on Main Street and bought a huge inflatable snowman, and stuck him next to our mailbox. "Looks good for the first attempt at a Scott family Christmas," I said.

We stared at our snowman and twinkling house, hoping that we blended in.

At lunch on Monday in the Venice High cafeteria, Colin and I sat at a table with Mackenzie and Fred. We tried to act natural, but I couldn't stop smiling at Colin. I felt like we were sharing a secret.

"So are you officially boyfriend-girlfriend now?" Mackenzie asked me in music class.

"I don't know." I stared at the floor. "I don't think we are. But how would I know?"

"You can see if he starts calling you his girlfriend to other people," Mackenzie said. She shrugged. "I don't know." Mackenzie had never had an official boyfriend either. "Or you can just ask him what your status is."

"What do I say—'Hey, am I your girlfriend?' What if he says no? That would be pathetic."

"True." She paused. "Speaking of not knowing your status—just before lunch Fred asked me if I wanted to go for a ride in Chester's carriage."

"Wow. Like a date?" Fred and Mackenzie had been friends for a long time, and even went to the Sadie Hawkins dance together in October, but it had never turned romantic. "Do you *like* him?"

She nodded and smiled. "I think I do."

I squeezed her hand. "Chester's getting a lot of business lately. Just don't get him started on the history of the horse and carriage—you'll never get a word, or a kiss, in edgewise."

We laughed. Mrs. Oderkirk, our music teacher, shushed us, and we joined the round of "Jingle Bells" that the class was singing off-key.

"Caroling rehearsals start tonight and continue weekly through Christmas," Mrs. Oderkirk told us as class ended. "Meet at five at Bea Sellers's house on Main and Picadilly—everyone's welcome! Especially baritones, if you know any!"

"How often do they go around caroling?" I asked Mackenzie as we left class.

"They don't come all the way out to our farm, thankfully, but I hear as Christmas approaches they go out every night."

"Thankfully?"

"It can get kind of old after a while. Just wait till you've sung 'Jingle Bells' every day in class until Christmas."

"I get the idea." I'd never even seen a single caroler in our neighborhood in Queens. Probably because no one wanted *Shut the ---- up!* yelled at them.

"Call me later and let me know what happens with Fred and the carriage," I told her as we approached the front entrance. Colin stood by the doors, waiting for me.

"Do you want a ride home?" he asked.

"Sure," I said. I bounced on my heels, and tried to quell the gymnasts springing around in my stomach.

Mackenzie raised her eyebrows and grinned. "Talk to you later," she said. I hugged her good-bye and walked with Colin to his car.

"I was thinking we could take a roundabout route," he said as we got in. "There's a place I want to take you to."

"What kind of place?" *A make-out hideaway? A place where he could declare me to be his girlfriend, perhaps?*

"Just a, uh—a cool place," he said.

I left Sam a message that I would be home late, and we drove past cornfields and onto a dirt road that wound up a gently sloping hill. Indiana's not as flat as its

Midwestern reputation would have you think—there were hills and rolling fields. We drove past an abandoned farm, down another dirt road, and stopped at a clearing by an old stone house.

"It's private property, so we're not exactly supposed to be here," Colin said. "Only a few people in town know about it. It's been abandoned as long as I can remember, but I heard someone in town inherited it. I don't know who, though."

We got out of the car and explored the grounds. A stone pathway led up to the house. It looked like it had been abandoned for years; the shutters were closed and a padlock hung on the front door. Tall trees edged the front yard, but beyond them the property ended—we came to the edge of a cliff. A magnificent view of the town lay below us.

"It's beautiful," I said.

It was almost four, and the sky was beginning to darken. The houses and trees on Main Street shimmered like stars.

I started to shiver. I had a hat in my pocket but I was worried it would look goofy if I put it on.

Colin took off his scarf and wrapped it around me. He reached for my hand.

"Soph, I know we haven't really talked about... what's happened. Since I kissed you."

"I—I know." Would this be a good time to pipe in with *Am I your girlfriend?* I felt so nervous I started babbling. "Sam's so worried about us that she gave me this book with chickens and farm animals doing it—I mean mating, and stuff—because she's scared that we might—not that you would—not that I don't want—" I finally stopped myself. What was wrong with me?

Colin smiled. "I'm happy to take things slow. I don't want to rush things and mess everything up."

I nodded.

He stared at the view. "Maybe we should just...see how things go with us."

"See how things go," I repeated.

I stared at dead grass on the lawn; I was happy and depressed at the same time. He did want to keep seeing me, but *see how things go*? It seemed so...realistic. In movies they never said *See how things go*. Mr. Darcy did not say *See how things go* to Elizabeth in *Pride and Prejudice*. It was assumed there would be a happily-ever-after.

What did I want him to say? Did I want him to pledge his undying love for me forever? I think I kind of did.

"What's wrong?" he asked. "Did I say the wrong thing?"

"No—I agree with you," I said. "A relationship is work. I know that." I didn't actually know that; it was something my mother used to say years ago, about being married to my father.

I squeezed his hand. Friendship seemed so simple in comparison: it is what it is. It was scary how uncertain this was. This was the cloudy uncharted future. He could change his mind about me at any minute. We could see how things go and then have them go awfully.

* * *

"Bah humbug," Sam said when I got home. "That's all I have to say: bah humbug."

"What are you bah humbugging?"

She perched on the sofa and motioned with her arms as she spoke. "I've never seen such a Christmas-crazy town before! You can't avoid it anywhere—at least in New York there are enough non-Christians around ignoring Christmas, but here every single person is celebrating it. Gus and I were trying to have a leisurely lunch at the Petal today when we were accosted by Bea Sellers of the Rose Society, who is just dying for Gus to join the caroling group. Apparently they need a baritone, and also, apparently, he can sing."

"Gus can sing? You're kidding."

"Turns out he had a drunken night of crooning about a year ago and word spread that he can sing. Of course he denies it wholeheartedly."

"He's never going to join them."

"That's what I thought at first. But she offered to pay him."

"Who pays Christmas carolers?"

"It's supply and demand—they need a baritone." She shook her head. "This was interesting, though—after Bea Sellers finally left us alone, Wilda came over to our table and gave Gus a loaf of cranberry bread she'd made just for him. With a pink ribbon around it. She told him, 'I had a great time last night.'" Her imitation of Wilda's voice sounded like a breathy femme fatale.

"I guess they had a *date*."

"Gus was really embarrassed about it," she said,

shaking her head. "He turned bright red, changed the subject, and didn't want to talk to me about it at all. Hey, speaking of budding romance, how was your afternoon?"

"What?"

She folded her arms. "How was your afternoon with Colin?"

I bit my lip. "Uh...um...good. How did you know?"

"Your face is flushed and glowy and you look like you just ate a whole bowl of candy. I'm not even going to ask what you were doing because I know I need to start trusting you two—at least that's what Josh says—even though you are my only sister in the whole entire world and I'm the only person watching out for you." She paused for half a second. "But you're fifteen and I can't keep a leash on you, even though I'd like to, but Josh says that would be cruel."

"Thank God for Josh," I said. "But you really don't need to worry. We talked about it tonight and we're taking it really slow—that's what he wants."

Sam smiled. "Now I remember why I like Colin."

On Friday night Colin and I went to see *It's a Wonderful Life* at Fred's theater. Afterward, we went with Mackenzie and Fred to the Petal Diner for dessert. Mackenzie had told me that the night before she and Fred had gone on the carriage ride, but hadn't yet kissed. From the way Fred was staring at her admiringly, though, I was pretty certain he wanted to.

"The one thing that bothers me about that movie is

the scene where they find out Mary's become a librarian. I mean they say, 'She's working at the library'—ahhh! Key the horror music! They make it sound like she's reached the saddest rung of humanity. Is being a librarian really such a horrible fate?" Mackenzie asked.

"Librarians get a bad rap," I said.

Colin agreed. "It's a great movie, Fred, but do you have to show it every single weekend? I mean, can't you mix it up with *Miracle on 34th Street* or *Scrooge* or something?"

"*It's a Wonderful Life* is the best Christmas movie there is. No other one compares. I'm a purist," he said.

After she'd cleared our dessert plates, Wilda, who nearly always wore pink, red, or a pastel yellow, disappeared for a few minutes, then came downstairs dressed in black pants and a black sweater.

I did a double take. She looked the way I had when I'd first come to Venice. I looked down at what I was wearing now—a white T-shirt, red sweater, and blue jeans. Slowly the all-black-wearing New Yorkness was seeping out of me—I'd recently even bought some pink clothes, too. My old friends from New York would drop their jaws if they could see me now.

"I'm just trying this on to get your opinion of what I should wear in L.A. when I visit my daughter for Christmas," Wilda said.

"I think they do wear colors out there," Mackenzie said.

"My daughter's always wearing black when I see her. I just want to look sophisticated," Wilda said. "Do I look sophisticated?"

"You look great," I said, and everyone nodded. "It's too bad you'll be gone for the holiday."

"Well, you'll all be together—you'll have a great time," Wilda said, picking lint off her outfit.

"Actually, I just found out yesterday we're going to Seattle for Christmas vacation. My aunt and cousins were supposed to come here, but my aunt is sick with something or other, so now we have to truck out there." Mackenzie rolled her eyes. "My cousins drive me crazy. They think we're hicks because we live in the Midwest. 'Want a latte? Oh wait, do you know what a latte is?'" she mimicked.

"I'll be in Muncie," Fred said. "Fun fun fun."

I looked at Colin. "Well, then it'll just be us—me and you and Sam."

He looked uncomfortable.

"I thought—you just went to London for Thanksgiving. I thought you said you don't go for both holidays." I gazed at him.

"I usually don't, but my dad really wants me to come. He said it's really important to him."

I didn't even realize how much I'd been looking forward to spending the holiday with them until now. Even though we hadn't celebrated Christmas in our old lives in Queens, we'd still spent the day with our friends. Viv, my best friend in New York, was from a Korean Buddhist family, and Sam's friend Felix was a firm atheist. Usually the four of us went to the movies on Christmas day—it was a fun tradition, and I guessed that a part of me had been expecting to do something similar with my friends here. Especially with Colin.

"Then it's just going to be me and Sam here without you all. That's not very *It's a Wonderful Life*-y, without our friends—I mean, what if I want to jump off a bridge or something?" I asked.

"Don't jump off a bridge," Mackenzie said.

"I might have to if you're all gone."

"Gus will be here," Wilda said. "And Fern, too."

I had a vision of Sam and me sitting in Gus's apartment, eating Gus's favorite Stouffer's frozen entrées, or spending Christmas with Fern, who worked in the administration office at Venice High, and her dog, Isabel.

"Eh, it's not a big deal," I said. But it was. I knew that part of what was bothering me was the glaring absence of our parents. Even though Christmas wasn't our holiday, I couldn't help but feel like I was becoming dangerously close to some depressing orphan character in a Dickens novel.

The others must have sensed my disappointment, because there was an awkward pause and then Wilda changed the subject.

"Maybe this will cheer you up," Wilda said. "That recipe you showed me how to make—that dumpling soup? Well, I changed it around a little, added a few things here and there, and I submitted it under our names to the *Griffin on the Go* annual recipe contest! I mean, it probably won't win"—she laughed—"but wouldn't it be exciting if it did? Then you and I could be on TV!"

"That sounds great," I lied, feeling even worse. The prospect of being on TV when you're a runaway wanted by your creepo stepmother for stealing thousands of dollars isn't too cheering. Not that an eggy sesame-flavored glueball had any chance of winning whatsoever.

"What's the recipe?" Mackenzie asked.

"The most delicious Ritz cracker–dumpling soup," Wilda said. "One thing though—I did change the recipe around a little bit—I hope you don't mind. I just thought, well, if I added some butter and a little flour and yeast, it would be that much better."

My mouth fell open. "Butter?" I asked. *"Yeast?"* I started coughing. Mackenzie patted me on the back.

"I'm sorry," Wilda said. "I know it was your ma's recipe—I shouldn't have changed it."

"No, your version sounds great—it doesn't matter," I said as I pictured legions of rabbis turning over in their graves: matzo-ball soup was served during Passover, when you weren't supposed to eat anything with yeast in it. And butter, when used with the turkey broth, wasn't kosher, either.

"They sound delicious," Colin said as I sank down in my seat.

"Matzo balls with butter and yeast?" Sam asked incredulously when I'd told her the story at home. She shook her head.

"They must be very fluffy," I said.

"What would Mommy think?"

"She'd probably think it was pretty funny. I hope."

Sam looked a little nervous.

"Don't worry," I said. "There's no way it's going to win. I'm sure they get a gazillion entries."

"You're right." She nodded.

"And how much could butter and yeast really help a dumpling made out of Ritz crackers?"

She smiled. "Good point. Adding sesame seeds to the recipe sounded pretty gross—and butter and yeast sound even worse."

"Wilda's just lucky if whoever tests the recipe doesn't get a stomachache."

"Or a permanent injury."

"Or a serious phobia about ruined-yeasted-icky pseudo matzo balls."

We laughed, and decided to forget about it. "Anyway, I've got more important things to worry about," I said. "Like final exams, and what I'm going to get Colin for Christmas." I flopped onto the couch.

"Any ideas yet?"

I shook my head. "None, and I have even less time to figure it out now, since he's leaving soon. I want it to be a good gift, but not something that says 'I'm expecting to marry you' and all that. It has to be a 'see how things go' gift."

"I don't know what a 'see how things go' gift would be," she said. "A toolbox? A nice hammer?"

I shrugged.

"Just get him some Old Spice." That's what she'd always gotten for our dad.

"I'm not getting him Old Spice. That's cheesy."

Her face fell.

"Oh my God, please tell me you didn't get Josh Old Spice," I said.

"They had a really nice gift set at the mall."

"I hope it's returnable," I said.

She sighed. "Now I don't know what to get him."

The night before Colin had to leave for London, we drove back to the overlook. There was a light snow on the ground; the stone house looked like it was frosted with powdered sugar. We stood on the ledge and stared down at Venice.

"I wish you weren't going," I said.

"Me, too. I'll be back in a week, though, and we can spend New Year's together." He reached into his coat pocket and pulled out a small box wrapped in silver paper. *For Sophie* had been written on the wrapping. "This is for you." He pressed it into my palm.

"I have something for you, too," I said, waving toward his car, where, in my book bag, I'd stashed a top-of-the-line hammer wrapped in pink tissue paper. I fingered the tiny silver box he'd given me. "Should I open it now, or save it till Christmas?"

"Open it now," he said.

I tore off the wrapping and opened the box. I took a deep breath. "Oh, wow. Wow." It was an antique silver locket engraved with tiny flowers on the front. The back was engraved with *For SS from CW*. My mouth felt dry. This was not a "see how things go" gift.

"I thought you could put pictures of your parents in it, or your sister," he said.

My throat tightened. "My mom used to wear one just like this with pictures of Sam and me inside it. It disappeared when she died. We never saw it again."

"It got lost in the accident?"

I'd forgotten our story for a moment, then remembered. I nodded. I fingered the locket, and he put it on me and fastened the clasp around my neck. I couldn't believe that he'd given me a gift that was so beautiful and sweet and heartfelt. And I'd gotten him a hammer.

"I don't know what to say," I said. Maybe this meant that on the "see how things go" front, things were going pretty well.

I kissed him with the lights of Venice winking below us, until I started to shiver from the cold. We went back to sit in his car.

I bit my lip. Should I delay giving him his present, and get him something better when he got back from London? But he was sitting in the front seat expectantly. He glanced at my book bag.

"And here's a little something for you," I finally said. I tried to sound cheerful, and took his present out and handed it to him. It felt like it weighed about ten pounds.

"Doesn't feel like a *little* something," he said. "I wonder what it is." He unwrapped it. He paused. "Wow. Nice hammer."

"Because you're crafty—you know? I wanted to get something useful. I mean—I love the locket. I guess I was afraid, I mean, I didn't want to get something that would say the wrong thing . . . "

"Huh?"

"I mean I didn't want you to think I'm rushing things. I thought the hammer was a good nonrushing gift."

"I like it. It's a great hammer."

"I guess I should have engraved it. Here—I'll take it back, I'll get it engraved—"

He laughed. "You don't need to engrave the hammer," he said "I love it." And we kissed until the windows fogged up in the car.

That night was also the first night of Chanukah, and when Colin dropped me off at home, Sam was arranging nine scented candles in a row.

"I waited for you to get home to light them," Sam said. "It's a bit more Pottery Barn than menorah, but whatever." One of the things we'd kept when we'd left Queens was our grandmother's heirloom menorah, the traditional candleholder used on Chanukah, but it was hidden under floorboards in our upstairs hall, along with other items that could reveal who we really were.

"What's that?" She pointed at the locket around my neck.

I fingered it. "It's a Christmas present from Colin."

"It looks like Mommy's."

"I know. I can't believe he gave it to me." I showed her the back of it with our initials engraved.

"So how did he like the hammer?" she asked.

I grunted and slumped into the sofa. "I can't believe I gave him a hammer. He pretended to like it, but it wasn't exactly romantic."

She searched around for matches. "I hope Josh likes the books I got him." She'd ordered him three books from Amazon. "It's hard to get gifts for guys. Old Spice, books, hammers—who knows what makes them happy?"

I shrugged.

"Josh is coming over in an hour," Sam said. "He said he's bringing us dinner—you didn't eat yet, did you?"

"No, I didn't." I'd been too busy kissing Colin to even think about food.

"He and Leo are leaving tomorrow for Chicago, to spend the holiday break with Josh's parents."

I felt a pang at the thought of celebrating Chanukah with family, and the pang worsened as we lit the center candle and the one for the first night. Then we sang the prayer and "Moaz Tzur," a Chanukah song that our mom had taught us. I tried to push the feelings away— Chanukah was a long holiday, and there were seven more days of this. I thought of Colin instead, and touched my locket.

Josh arrived an hour later with a huge platter covered in tinfoil. "Hope you're hungry," he said. The platter was filled with latkes, applesauce, sour cream, and a heap of brisket and green beans. "Don't worry, I didn't rob a deli—the Wilshire College dining service made this big feast tonight. They try to be all-inclusive about holiday food, but there were hardly any students around to enjoy it since almost everyone's left for break already. So I got all this to go."

We set the table and dug in. It was a little awkward eating the latkes, since even though Josh and his grandfather, Leo, knew our secret, Sam still liked to pretend that they didn't know. I think it made her feel more secure to keep up the charade. Obviously Sam and I knew what latkes were, and that it was Chanukah, but Sam

wouldn't want us to admit it in the open. So we just ig-
nored the subject altogether; Josh nodded at the row of
candles on our mantel, only the middle and one end one
lit, but didn't mention anything about it.

He made us laugh with stories of Wilshire students
going crazy during final exam week—a freshman running naked across the campus; students putting their
dogs on cross-country skis; people wearing the same
pajamas for five days straight. Then he pulled out three
small boxes tied with ribbon from his knapsack.

"These are for you two, from Leo," he said, and
handed two of the boxes to us.

He placed the third present under our tree. "And this
is for you, Sam—but you can't open it until Christmas."
Josh grinned. He was teasing her with this whole
Christmas thing. I suppressed a laugh, and Sam and I
opened Leo's gifts.

It was a box of eight exquisite-looking handmade
chocolates.

"Ruth Brauner made them," Josh said. "She's been
making them out of her house. Leo's trying to convince
her to start a little business." Ruth was Leo's first love,
who we'd helped him find—it was our second missing
person case after we'd moved to Venice.

I ate one of the chocolates, which was filled with
caramel; it was delicious and melted on my tongue.
"These are amazing. I'm going to have one for each night
of...until they're gone." I caught myself. "You'll have to
thank Ruth and Leo for us," I said.

"I will," Josh said, laughing.

"I have something for you, too," Sam told him, and got out her gifts for Josh. He loved the books she'd gotten him—*Armchair Economist, Hidden Order: The Economics of Everyday Life,* and the complete *Lord of the Rings* trilogy. When he picked up her hand to thank her I realized I should leave them alone.

"I'll let you two go the way of the chickens," I told my sister.

She made a face. "We're not—"

"Good night," I said, and hugged Josh good-bye. He whispered "Happy Chanukah" in my ear.

Before I went to bed, I wrote in my journal everything that had happened that night, and touched Colin's locket around my neck. I pictured him on his flight to London—surely not clutching my hammer. I decided I'd get him a better present soon, and fell asleep.

The next morning I woke up to the phone ringing. It was Mackenzie calling from the Indianapolis airport; she and her family were waiting for their flight to Seattle to board.

"I'm sorry to call so early but I had to tell you—Fred kissed me last night," she said.

"Wow! How was it?" I asked.

"Good. He's, well—he's a good kisser. But get this. When we said good-bye, guess what he told me?"

"What?"

"See you."

"Oh no. Please tell me you're kidding."

"Nope. I'm not."

We started laughing and then they called her flight. "Merry Christmas," she said.

"You, too." We hung up.

I got out of bed. Sam was getting dressed. "Want to get breakfast at the Petal? Wilda's only serving four more meals before she leaves for L.A." The diner was going to be closed for all of Christmas week.

"Let's go," I said. I got dressed, and Sam and I put on our coats and walked to the Petal.

"What are we going to eat for the next week?" I asked Sam as we trudged down Main Street.

She shrugged. "I don't know. We're going to starve. At least we don't need to worry about gaining weight over the holidays."

We were about to walk into the diner when, through the middle of the massive wreath on the door, I saw a man in a black hat and gray suit talking to Officer Alby in a booth. I squinted at him; he looked familiar.

I'd seen him before. Something sour rose in my throat.

I ducked and grabbed Sam's arm. "That's Hertznick! *Run!*"

Four

"Oh God, oh God, we're screwed—we're dead," I babbled as Sam led me into the It's Christmas! store across the street. "We have to get home before he comes out of there," I pleaded with her.

She clutched my arm. "We need to find out what's going on—what's Alby telling him?" Her voice wavered. We hid behind a huge fake Christmas tree and watched the diner through the store windows.

"We're toast," I whispered, shaking my head. I bumped into a monstrous plastic reindeer behind me. "Hertznick is telling everyone who we are *right now*. We need to go home and get in the car and *leave*." My voice cracked.

"Not yet—we can't panic yet," she said, though she scrunched up her face, which was as red as a tomato.

I didn't even know if Hertznick would recognize us in our winter outfits—down jackets with thick hats and earmuffs; I pulled my hat down over my head even more. "What if he comes in here?" I asked.

"We can't go home," she said. "Alby could take him to our house. Just give me a second. I need to think." Sam looked really worried.

A moment later, the door to the diner opened and

Hertznick and Alby stepped out. They headed in different directions down Main Street.

I clutched Sam's hand. "Where's he going? What do we do?"

Before we could make a decision, the door of the diner opened again, and this time Fern came out. She headed straight toward the It's Christmas! store.

Sam and I fled to the back of the shop and ducked behind another enormous tree dripping with garlands and toy-soldier ornaments. I was sure if she saw us she'd say: "There you are! The Shattenberg girls! Do you know a detective from New York is looking for you? I always knew you were faking..." We watched her inspect the tinsel display.

Then she spotted us.

"Hi, dears! Have you seen this tinsel? It's half off."

We nodded nervously.

"Are you girls okay? You don't look so good. Maybe you should take your hats off? It's kind of warm in here." She took off her scarf.

"Yeah," Sam said, keeping her hat on. Her face was still bright red.

"I'm just doing some last-minute Christmas shopping," Fern said, examining one of the toy soldiers. "I had breakfast at the Petal—only a few more meals left now till Wilda closes for Christmas. You should head over there—she's got some great sticky buns."

We stayed silent, frozen in our places.

She laughed suddenly. "You won't believe it but there was some weirdo in there—some acquaintance of

Alby's—his name was Kapertnik or something. Anyway, he said he was from New York City and was looking for some runaway druggie criminal girls." She rolled her eyes.

"Druggies?" Sam asked.

"Drug dealers. That's what I heard." She shrugged. "As if we wouldn't notice drug dealers invading our town! Please." She shook her head. "I bet he's the criminal—I read in the *Enquirer* that people like that come to small towns and get people scared and then take advantage of them." She nodded knowingly.

Did Hertznick think we'd become drug dealers? Where did he get that idea? My shoulders relaxed a little at the fact that she hadn't figured out who we were. I breathed deeply. But Hertznick was on the loose—we had to get home somehow without running into him.

"Well, I better get going—I've got loads of Christmas shopping to do. See you, girls! Going to pay for my tinsel!" Fern said, waving a bag of glittery silver stuff at us. Sam and I said good-bye and pretended to look for more ornaments for our tree.

Then I thought of something—I'd been in such a panic it hadn't even occurred to me before. "Colin's shop," I whispered to Sam. "We can go there—he's already left for London and he told me where he keeps a key, in case of an emergency while he's gone."

We wrapped our scarves around our faces so that only our eyes were visible as we walked, trying not to look suspicious. We took a roundabout route and kept an eye out for Hertznick. We didn't see him. I picked up

Colin's key from under a ceramic goose in the backyard, and we opened the back door.

It was strange to be in Colin's shop without him there. The heat had been turned down; it was freezing and looked so dark and empty.

Sam had left our cell phone at home, so we called Difriggio, our Midwestern criminal adviser, on Colin's phone. We used a calling-card number so it wouldn't appear on his bill. I got on the extension.

After releasing a string of expletives, Difriggio said, "I didn't plant that drug-dealer thing—I don't know where he heard that from. And I don't know how he found his way to Venice—I thought Hertznick had given up on Indiana. Who was he talking to in the diner?"

"Officer Alby," I said.

"It's possible that Alby contacted him," Difriggio said.

My tone darkened. "How could Alby have figured us out and tracked down Hertznick? He's not that smart..."

"Let's hope he's not," Difriggio said. Sam told him about Fern not making the connection.

"You've gotten real lucky. But depending on how many people Hertznick and Alby spoke to, someone's gonna figure it out."

A sob leaked out of me. This was it. Our new lives were over. I glanced around the shop desperately, as if I was looking for a way to stop time, or to erase the last hour.

Difriggio sighed. "I'm going to try to set up a new gig for you girls. I've got a contact in Tucson."

"Tucson?" Sam asked.

"Tucson, Arizona. We might have to go with that, or a smaller town in the state, like Yuma or Bisbee."

Yuma? Bisbee? I'd never even heard of those places. My body felt like it was going to collapse. How could I leave Colin? I finally had a sort-of boyfriend for the first time in my life and I was going to have to run away to Yuma.

"Stay put until I can set things up," Difriggio said. "And in the meantime I'm going to send a guy to Venice to trail Hertznick. I'll give you a call when Hertznick's left town."

We gave him the number at Colin's and hung up. I buried my face in my hands. "Why?" I moaned. "Why can't we just get a break?"

Sam shook her head.

We spent the next few hours hiding in the shop, trying not to go crazy with panic while we waited for Difriggio to call us back. I sat in Colin's chair and glanced at the notes on his desk beside the cash register from the last week: *Antique watches—50 cents, call Tues. Pressed flower xmas tree ornaments—pickup Mon.* I started to look through the other notes around—I don't know what I was hoping to find—a Post-it scrawled with *Colin loves Sophie*? *Colin and Sophie 4ever, even if she has to move to Yuma*? But it gave me a little thrill to look, and took my mind off our situation.

"What are you doing, looking for a love note?" Sam asked.

"No." I tried to sound innocent.

"Come look at this." She held up a photo album she'd taken off a shelf in the back. It was filled with photos of Colin's family. We sat on the sofa and pored through it, and I lost myself for a while in those pictures—Colin as a kid with the same dark brown bangs he had now; Colin on his dad's shoulders by the canal, and with his mom in the park. I'd never seen a picture of his mom before—she was beautiful, with long black hair that cascaded down her back. We saw photos of her pushing Colin on a swing, and sitting with him in the gazebo on Main Street, and in front of the Indianapolis Children's Museum. I hoped Colin wouldn't mind us looking at the album. It made me feel closer to him, even though he was thousands of miles away.

Difriggio finally called us three hours later, and said Hertznick had been tracked to a hotel in Indianapolis. He had a flight out at five P.M. that day, to go to Boca Raton for the holidays. Difriggio would have someone make sure that he got on that flight.

We were afraid to leave our house and return to the diner—we worried that someone would tell us they recognized us from what Hertznick had said, and turn us in. So we avoided it completely. On Sunday morning Wilda called us.

"Where are you two? I'm leaving this afternoon and I've been waiting for you to come by. I just closed up the diner and I've got some leftovers for you to take home. And I was hoping you could look in on Betty while I'm gone."

"Of course," I said. "No problem."

We agreed to meet Wilda in her apartment in an hour. When we arrived she was all packed and ready to go, and was writing a long note on pink paper.

"Fern said she'd take care of Betty, too, but I think Betty really likes you girls better. You're cat people," Wilda said.

Sam made a face. She had come to love Zayde, but the words *cat person* seemed more fitting for the old woman on our block in Queens who had about forty of them.

"These are just a few pointers," Wilda explained, showing us the two-page list. "I left a plate of cooked chicken in the fridge which should last a couple days, but then you'll have to give her Fancy Feast after that. On Christmas Day, though, please take a chicken breast out of the freezer and defrost it; here are directions on how to cook it the way she likes it, okay? I want Betty to have a nice Christmas." She petted her cat, who was sitting on a chair, absorbed in licking herself. "And I cued *Four Weddings and a Funeral* in the VCR—she loves that movie. If you could put it on when you leave, she'll feel like she has company."

"Sure," Sam said warily, gazing at Wilda as if she was insane.

"How were the last few meals at the diner?" I asked Wilda. "I'm sorry we missed them—we've just been so busy with Christmas shopping." She didn't seem like she made any connection with Hertznick whatsoever, but I thought it couldn't hurt to try to find out.

"I almost forgot—I put these aside for you." She took

out two pans of food and two pies from her fridge. "We had one oddball in yesterday—some friend of Alby's. Some people overheard he was looking for drug dealers, but I'm sure it's baloney. Probably some new scheme Alby's conjuring up." A month ago, Alby had tried to make himself seem like a better policeman by stealing pets around town and then returning them to their owners. Naturally, his plan had backfired. But maybe what had happened was working in our favor— maybe no one would believe Alby if he voiced any suspicions. At least that's what I hoped.

There was a knock on the door.

"Ready?" Gus asked Wilda as he opened the door. Then he saw us. He blinked with surprise. "Oh. Hi," he said. "Just, uh, giving Wilda a ride to the airport. Our flights leave around the same time."

"Flights?" Sam asked. "I thought you were staying here."

"I thought I told you," he said.

We shook our heads.

"I, uh—I'm leaving, too. I'm going to see Jack in Vegas." He stared down at the floor; he seemed embarrassed that he and Wilda obviously had something going on.

"It was my idea," Wilda said. "I convinced him to go see Jack, even though Bea Sellers is going to kill me since they don't have a baritone. Gus had to give her her money back!"

Gus glanced at his watch. "We better get going."

We hugged Wilda good-bye, and then Gus. "Happy

holidays," Gus said to us. "I'm sorry I won't be here with you."

"We'll be fine," Sam said. "Say hi to Jack. Don't gamble too much."

"Bye, Betty," Wilda said, and kissed her cat about ten times. Gus sighed audibly, and then picked up her suitcase, which was hot pink and embroidered with the face of a grinning tabby, and trotted down the stairs.

The holidays are a really lovely time of year when you're orphaned, about to leave all your loved ones and your home for the second time, and your only company is your depressed sister and your asthmatic cat. The days had been dragging by.

"'Twas the night before Christmas, and visions of the Witness Protection Program danced through their heads," my sister chanted drily while we surfed through the TV channels for the third day in a row. Outside, the carolers were singing "Winter Wonderland." When they finished, Bea Sellers announced, "I apologize for the lack of a baritone." They moved on to the next house.

It was also the sixth night of Chanukah, so Sam and I each had another one of Ruth's chocolates, then exchanged our gifts—the Chanukah tradition was to exchange one gift each night—but we couldn't even really enjoy it, with everything that was weighing on us. So far she'd gotten me a mechanic's tool kit, a new guitar stand, sheet music, a Nancy Drew calendar, the video of *I Capture the Castle,* and tonight, a huge assortment of mini-nail polishes. I'd gotten her a subscription to *The*

Nation, a facial cleansing kit since she had no skin-care regimen whatsoever, clothes, and tonight, a set of Sherlock Holmes radio plays on CD.

"Twenty hours of Sherlock Holmes," Sam read off the label. We watched *Miracle on 34th Street* while I painted each of my toenails black. "They're bah humbug toe-nails," I explained to Sam.

"Hey, since it's Christmas Eve I can open Josh's gift, too, right?" Sam asked, perking up a little.

"Sure," I said. "Christmas Eve, Christmas Day, same diff."

She tore open Josh's gift: a silver charm bracelet with charms of an ear of corn, an S, an open book, and a heart. She tried calling him to thank him, but got no an-swer. I hadn't spoken to Colin either; he'd left two mes-sages since he'd gone to London, and I'd missed his calls both times.

As the voices of the carolers came around for the sec-ond time—only in Venice did they get to do the whole town twice—Sam and I stayed up late listening to the Sherlock Holmes radio plays in her room.

"What are you thinking?" Sam asked me, when we'd finished listening to "Silver Blaze," our father's favorite story.

"I don't want to go to Arizona," I said.

"Neither do I," she said.

We both fell asleep on her bed, though I kept waking up with thoughts of Hertznick, Arizona, and Colin. Zayde slept between us, snoring through the night, getting more rest than either Sam or I did.

We were awoken Christmas morning by our doorbell ringing.

"Who's that?" Sam's voice growled. She squinted at me.

"Whaa?"

The doorbell kept ringing.

"Don't get it," I said suddenly, clearing my throat. "It could be Hertznick!"

"Hertznick's in Florida," she said, and peeked out the window. "I don't see anybody out there."

"Maybe it's Santa. Maybe he delivers all the presents to the Jews-pretending-to-be-Christians last."

We put on our bathrobes and stood at the top of the stairs as the doorbell kept buzzing.

"You think we should get it?" I asked Sam.

Then we heard a voice with a thick New York accent.

"Hello!! Anyone in there?! You sure we got the right address?" The *sure* sounded like "shawr."

Sam and I grinned and raced toward the door. I knew that voice well—it belonged to Viv, my best friend from New York.

Five

"OH MY GAWD!!" Viv yelled as I was enveloped in a cloud of black leather jacket, black scarf, and black hair. "OH MY GAWD!!"

Felix loped toward my sister and wrapped his arms around her.

"What are you guys doing here?!" Sam shouted. I kept hugging Viv and laughing, and before I knew it, my eyes had welled up and I couldn't even speak. I hadn't known if I'd ever see her again, and here she was, hugging me.

"I checked with Difriggio and he said it was okay," Felix said. "But we can't stay long and we can't leave the house, and there are about fifteen other rules Difriggio gave me, too," he said as we kept hugging. Felix ran a fake-ID business out of his basement; he'd helped us secure our new identities and had hooked us up with Difriggio. He ran his hand through his hair and wiped off his glasses. "I can't believe we made it. We've been on the road for eleven hours."

I glanced at the clock—it was ten A.M. "You left last night?"

"Yeah. I'm actually pretty wired, though, after five cups of coffee!" Viv said, looking around our living room.

"Wow, you got a Christmas tree? What are those brown things hanging off it?"

"Ferrets," I said. "Long story. I'll explain later."

"Who needs sleep?" Felix said. "We're here!"

"It's actually kinda hard to sleep when someone's blasting Neil Diamond songs," Viv said, rolling her eyes at Felix.

"'Turn on Your Heartlight' is one of the greatest masterpieces of all time," Felix said.

Viv shook her head.

"I can't believe Difriggio said it was okay to come," Sam said. She gaped at our friends as if they were ghosts.

"He's been keeping me updated on you guys. He said you were real down and you might have to be moving again soon—I wanted to see you before you move another two thousand miles," Felix said. "Difriggio wasn't too happy about my idea of a visit, but I convinced him. I think he felt sorry for you guys."

I kept staring at Viv and shaking my head. "I just can't believe you're here. I just—" My throat dried up. "I didn't know if I'd ever see you again."

She hugged me again and touched my hair. "Look at you! You're all blond."

I'd forgotten that she hadn't seen me since the transformation. "Pretty weird, isn't it?"

"You look gawgeous."

Felix yawned. "I think I'm going to need another cup of coffee."

Sam led us into the kitchen and started to make a

pot. "Are you sure you're feeling okay? Do you need a nap?" she asked them.

They shook their heads. "No—I want to catch up," Viv said.

Felix sat down at the table. "Believe it or not, we can only stay twenty-four hours. We have to drive back tomorrow morning."

My heart sank at the thought of them leaving so soon. "But you just got here."

"I know, we're nuts," Viv said. "But this was our only chance to see you." She smiled. "The road trip was really fun. I've never been past New Jersey—who knew there was all this land out here?"

I smiled and shrugged. "Who knew?"

"What did you tell your families?" Sam asked. "Do they know you're here?"

"Of course not," Felix said. "What do you take me for, an amateur? My aunt is in Manila for Christmas, so she thinks I'm at my cousins'. My cousins think I'm at Viv's."

"I'm staying at Rachel Horowitz's house in Brooklyn as far as my family knows," Viv said.

She looked around the kitchen and then walked into the living room, peering up the stairs. "God, check this place out. It's HUGE. Quilts and rocking chairs...it's like *Little House on the Prairie.*"

I laughed. Viv heard our cat coughing. "Did you get a dog?"

"No, that's our cat Zayde—she has asthma. The heat makes the air dry, so it's been acting up lately," I said.

I showed Viv my room upstairs, and we sat on my bed

and caught up on everything that had happened since I'd left Queens. She told me how she and Felix had become better friends since Sam and I'd run away, and I told her all about Mackenzie—I felt a little bad telling her about a new close friend—and about Colin. I showed her his picture from the Sadie Hawkins dance in the fall, and the locket he'd given me.

"He's adorable," she said. "They make them cute and sweet out here in the cornfields. Must be the fresh air or something. What is it with the guys at LaGuardia? Like it's cool to not wash your hair for two weeks and wear the same grungy jeans day after day." She sighed. "Maybe I should move here, too."

"I wish you could." I put the photo of Colin away. "Though who knows how much longer we'll be here. I might never see him again." I stared at the comforter and told her in detail all about Hertznick and Yuma.

"Maybe he'll pack up and move to Yuma with you. Or maybe Hertznick will get stuck on this drug-dealer thing and leave you alone here. Hey, guess who planted the drug-dealer rumor?" she asked.

"Who?"

"Felix and me. Hertznick was asking around at Science and LaGuardia. So I told some friends the rumor, and Felix hinted to some of his fake-ID buyers at Science that you were bringing drugs across the border from Mexico. The rumor spread and I guess Hertznick bought it." She shrugged with pride.

"Thanks for doing that," I said.

"Anytime."

We ate the food that Felix and Viv had brought—
bagels from H&H, knishes from Knish Nosh, and sweet-
rice-and-red-bean cakes from the Korean grocery on Fifty-
second Street in Queens. Viv had also brought an article
from the LaGuardia High School newspaper about my disappearance. It was weird to read about myself in the third
person, and the picture they'd run of me was hideous.
Enid must have dug it up from somewhere, since it was
about three years old. My eyes were shut, and I had
glasses and braces. "How embarrassing," I said.

"At least no one's going to recognize you with that
photo," she said. "Especially since you're now a glam-
orous blonde."

I laughed. She told me about Cyrus, a guy she met
who went to Stuyvesant, who she'd kissed twice. And
about her family's grocery store, and our old friends at
school, and the new shops that had opened near Lincoln
Center.

We talked for hours—when I looked at the clock it
was late afternoon. "Oh God—I've got to go cook our
friend's cat her Christmas dinner."

Viv squinted at me. *"What?"*

I explained about Wilda and Betty as I got dressed—
I'd been wearing my pajamas since they'd arrived—and
put on jeans and a pink sweater.

Viv blinked at me. "You're wearing PINK?"

"I know." I sighed. "I've lost my edge."

"Pink's a nice color, it's just that it seems to scream
'Mug me.' But you probably don't have to worry about
that here."

"Probably not," I said, smiling. We went downstairs to the kitchen, where Sam and Felix had been talking, and I reminded Sam about feeding Betty.

"Why don't you guys come with us?" Sam suggested. "We can give you a mobile tour of the town on the way." We didn't want to walk since we wanted to avoid running into anyone. But the streets looked completely deserted anyway.

"Well, I told Difriggio we'd stay in the house, but the car's kind of the same thing," Felix said with a sly shrug. "I won't tell him if you won't."

"We won't," I said.

"She's looking good," Felix said, patting the hood of our brown '78 Buick clunker before he got inside. Felix had gotten the car for us before we left Queens.

"Sophie took a mechanics class last semester," Sam said.

Viv blinked. "You're kidding me."

"I did—I swear." I whispered: "It was *all guys*." She nodded approvingly.

"Can't wait to see the sights," Felix said. "Where's the canal? We saw the signs for it on the highway."

"Oh," Sam groaned. "It's kind of a disappointment, but...well, let's get going."

We drove to the canal, got out of the car, and peered over the edge at the layer of dirty snow and random bits of garbage. There were even a few pigeons pecking around.

"Looks kinda like the subway tracks in Queens," Viv said. "At least you can come here when you feel homesick."

We drove to the back lot behind the Petal Diner and walked up the stairs to Wilda's apartment.

I followed Wilda's directions for cooking Betty's special Christmas chicken breast. Wilda had also left a strawberry pie in the freezer for us to heat up, so I cooked that, too, and we sat at Wilda's kitchen table eating, in true holiday style. Betty gulped down her chicken in about three minutes, and then sprawled happily across the heat vent and fell asleep.

On the way back home Felix and Viv started to fall asleep, too. At six o'clock Felix crashed on the downstairs couch and Viv went to bed in the spare room—and slept until early the next morning. Sam cooked eggs and French toast for breakfast, and as we ate I began to feel gloomy again.

"You can't leave," I said. "This was way too short. You have to stay longer..."

"Don't worry—we'll see each other again soon," Viv said. But her voice sounded sad; I wasn't sure if she meant it.

After breakfast they packed up their things; I started to cry as I hugged her good-bye. I wanted to believe that I'd see her soon, but I didn't know if I could.

"And you'll come back to the city sometime, right?" Viv said to me. "Or I'm going to have to apply to that Wilbert College."

"Wilshire," I said. "It's not a bad school. Maybe we can go there together if we're still here, and not in Yuma."

"I'll go to Yuma University if I have to, if it means we can be in the same place again," Viv said. We hugged for a long time. Sam and Felix hugged, too.

"Say hi to Queens for me," Sam said, her voice catching as Viv and Felix picked up their knapsacks and headed toward their car.

"We will."

Viv waved, and tried to smile. We watched them get into their car and drive away.

Wilda, Gus, and Mackenzie all returned on Sunday night, and Wilda reopened the diner first thing the next morning. Difriggio had been keeping tabs on Hertznick's whereabouts, and assured us that Hertznick was still in Boca Raton with his parents. We met Mackenzie at the Petal for breakfast.

Wilda was tanned from her visit to Los Angeles. "I had a good time, but I didn't see a single celebrity! I went to Melrose, Beverly Hills, Century City—finally Rosa took me to the wax museum, but it's not the same as seeing them in the flesh." She went into the kitchen and brought us blueberry pancakes.

The bells on the front door of the diner jingled, and Gus walked in. Sam and I got up to greet him.

"How was Vegas?" I asked.

"I lost twenty bucks on the nickel slots. Jack says hello. He's doing good. We managed to get through all that time with only two fights."

"Not bad," I said.

Wilda came over to our booth and squeezed Gus's shoulder. Sam and I exchanged glances and Gus turned pink.

Their romantic display was interrupted by a FedEx man traipsing through the diner with his clipboard.

Everyone looked up. FedEx deliveries were not a common occurrence in Venice.

"Miss Wilder Higgins?" the man asked.

"Oh, um, I guess that's me," Wilda said. "What could it be?" She looked nervous. "Who'd FedEx me something? I hope it's not bad news."

She signed for it and tore the envelope open. It contained a letter. Her eyes bulged as she read it.

"What is it?" I asked.

"Oh, my good sweet Lord. Holy mackerel! Holy bejeezus!"

Gus wrinkled his brow. Wilda looked like she was about to have a heart attack.

"What?" Sam asked.

"I'M GONNA BE ON TV!!" She pointed a finger at me. "AND SO ARE YOU!"

Six

"What?" everyone asked in unison. I sat there with my mouth open, completely speechless.

"It's from GourmetTV. That cable channel. That recipe Sophie showed me how to make—that dumpling soup? It won the *Griffin on the Go* contest! WE'RE GOING TO BE ON TV! GRIFFIN IS COMING TO VENICE!"

Wilda started bouncing up and down. I'd never seen her like this before. She kissed Gus squarely on the lips; he looked like he wanted to sink under the table.

She shook her head. "I just can't believe *Griffin on the Go* picked *our recipe*!" She sat down in a chair next to our booth and read the letter again. "It says they're going to come to Venice on Friday to tape the show here in the diner. I can't believe it."

My face grew hot; my stomach turned over. A year ago I would have been overjoyed to be on TV. Now, as a runaway criminal with a private detective after me, it was another story.

"Are you okay?" Mackenzie asked.

"Sophie has a phobia," Sam blurted. "A camera phobia." She nodded emphatically.

"What?" Wilda asked.

"She has a deadly fear of being on camera. I mean—remember that time in Cleveland when you almost got

on the news for that story about broken traffic lights?"
She touched my shoulder. "Sophie totally freaked out."

Where was Sam getting this stuff? She should join an
improv troupe. I went along with it and nodded. "Yeah,
it's true. It's really weird—I just get so nervous being on
camera—it freaks me out." I shrugged. Maybe we'd be
in Arizona by the time the TV crew got here, anyway. I
shifted in my seat. I didn't want that to happen, either.

"I've heard of phobias like that," Mackenzie said.
"My aunt Lisa is completely terrified by dogs. Even little
poodles."

"That's awful," Wilda said to me. "Can you seek help
for that kind of thing?"

"Sophie's tried," Sam said. "She's gone to two thera-
pists—but nothing's worked."

I shrugged. "Nope. Nothing."

"Well, maybe you can just see how you feel when
Griffin shows up. He seems like a very kind man on the
show—I bet he'll make you feel calm and relaxed. I just
can't believe Griffin *is* coming to Venice," Wilda said
again, breathily, gazing off into the distance.

Gus wrinkled his brow. "Let me see that." He looked
over the *Griffin on the Go* flyer that came with the letter;
it had a full-page photo of Griffin looking especially
dashing in a perfectly tailored suit, his chiseled features
and brooding face staring off into snowcapped Alps. He
looked like a movie star.

"Griffin Gaddux," Gus said, reading the poster.

"It's Gateaux, pronounced *Gateoou,*" Wilda cor-
rected. "It's French."

"Doesn't gâteau mean 'cake'?" Sam asked.

"Sure does. Beefcake," Mackenzie said, widening her eyes. We giggled.

"Don't tell me you really think that chump is good-looking," Gus said.

"He's a dreamboat," Wilda said. "But not as dreamy as you." She patted Gus's arm.

He grunted and looked away. I tried not to giggle again.

"It'll be good for the town—Venice could use the tourism boost," Wilda said.

Mackenzie nodded. "Griffin has tons of fans all over—my mom loves his show. She watches it all the time."

"I never heard of him," Gus said.

Wilda paused and read the letter for the tenth time. "It says the show is based out of New York City. Can you believe all these *New Yorkers* are coming to Venice?" She said "New Yorkers" as if it was a rare species.

"I know," Mackenzie said. "They're going to hate it here."

"Can you imagine?" Wilda asked. "Wares tha cawfee?" she said in the most non-New-Yorky attempt at a New York accent I'd ever heard.

Sam and I exchanged glances. What were we in for?

"I can't believe yeasted sesame Ritz cracker matzo balls are going to be on TV," Sam said as we walked home. "Is that show insane?"

"They're not matzo balls anymore," I said. "They're *dumplings*."

"Whatever they are, you're not going near that camera for any reason whatsoever."

"Of course I'm not. According to you, I have a deathly phobia of TV cameras. And why do I have that deathly phobia?"

"I don't know. You must have had a bad experience with a TV camera as a kid."

"Okay," I said. "Sure." I hoped everyone would believe that. I tried to imagine how I'd explain my camera phobia to Colin without him thinking I was a nutcase. I missed him so much—he was getting back on New Year's Eve, the day after next—I prayed Difriggio wouldn't call us suddenly and tell us we had to leave before I even saw Colin again. My stomach clenched at the thought of that.

We called Difriggio as soon as we got home. We thanked him for letting Felix and Viv come visit, and then he said, "I was just about to call you girls—I have good news."

I held my breath and hoped he wasn't about to say he'd found a great bungalow for us in Yuma.

"Hertznick got fired," Difriggio said. "The witch canned him."

"What?"

"Your stepmother, Enid Gutmyre, fired him. Apparently she got his latest bill and she refused to pay it. She thinks he's charging her too much money."

"Oh my God." I couldn't believe it. For the first time in a while I thought maybe, somehow, our parents actually *were* watching out for us.

"This means we can stay in Venice, right?" Sam asked.

He paused. "For now. She could hire another detective to pick up where Hertznick left off. But let's hope if she does it's someone not too good. Or maybe she'll give up altogether. But we can't count on that. Also, damage could've already been done from Hertznick's visit to Venice. You need to keep a real close eye out in case anyone's on to you. Especially Alby. I'm worried about what Hertznick might have said to him."

We told him that from everyone we'd talked to, it seemed that no one had made a connection based on Hertznick's visit.

"Still—be careful. Especially around Alby."

"But Alby's such a dimwit. I can't imagine him turning us in," Sam said.

"Don't discount him until you're certain. Avoid him as much as you can. I don't know—I'm still thinking about Tucson or Yuma for you, keeping it on the back burner."

Sam told him about the latest development, the TV show, and Difriggio thought in silence for a minute.

"Maybe it's not such a good time for you to leave right now at all, then," he said. "It'll look too suspicious with the television crew there. You're going to have to lay low. But whatever you do, don't get on camera," he warned me.

I promised I wouldn't.

On New Year's Eve, I picked up the phone for the hundredth time to check that there was a dial tone. I called

Colin at home, but his answering machine picked up. He didn't have a cell phone, so I couldn't try him that way, and he hadn't left a message for me since Christmas. I was worried. Had he changed his mind about me while he was away? Had something horrible happened to him?

"Don't worry, he'll be here any minute," Mackenzie said as we walked to Main Street for the town's New Year's festivities.

"His flight was supposed to get in at five." I glanced at my watch. It was ten o'clock.

"It probably just got delayed," she said.

Sam and Josh had gone out to dinner, and were supposed to meet us at the gazebo, but I didn't see them there yet.

It looked like all of Venice had come to the celebration. The Venice Elementary School marching band banged their drums and xylophones, and stands sold hot chocolate, eggnog, and apple cider doughnuts. As it neared midnight, Bea Sellers's carolers congregated in the gazebo and sang "Have a Holly Jolly New Year" and other Christmas carols with *New Year* stuck in where *Christmas* should be; Bea was conducting. I searched their faces—in the back of the crowd I spotted Gus, hitting the baritone notes.

"I can't believe it," I told Mackenzie. "He *can* sing."

Wilda joined us, clutching a cup of hot chocolate. "He's good, isn't he?"

We nodded. "How's everything going with you two?" I asked her.

"Good—but you know Gus. He seems to have a hard time publicly admitting that we're an item."

"Maybe he's seeing how things go," I said.

"Maybe," she said.

Mackenzie smiled at the reference.

They finished their round of songs and Nancy Weller, the mayor of Venice, took the microphone. I saw Bea slip Gus a twenty, and Gus came over to us.

"You were great," I told him.

"Eh." He shrugged.

Wilda hugged him while he squirmed, and then she squeezed my shoulder. "So are you excited? Griffin'll be here Friday—I can't wait," she said. "Do you really think your phobia will get in the way?"

"Actually I—I do." I stared down at the pavement. "I don't think I can do it," I told her.

"You'll see—once they're here and filming, you'll relax—you'll be wonderful on the show."

"I really can't do it," I repeated.

"Can't you just give it a little try?" Wilda asked.

"She can help out behind the scenes instead," Gus suggested.

"Definitely—I'll be there off camera," I said. "I'll help out that way." I was grateful to Gus for standing up for me.

"If that's really what you want," Wilda said. "I just don't want you to feel left out."

"I won't."

Sam and Josh joined us, and so did Fred and his dog, Herman. Fred passed out kazoos. He looked nervous as he hugged Mackenzie. He kissed her on the cheek awkwardly, and she blushed.

"Where's Colin? He's not back yet?" Sam asked me.

"He was supposed to be back hours ago. I'm really getting worried," I said. "I hope nothing's happened to him." I shrugged and tried to sound nonchalant, but my mind began to spin off with different scenarios—a plane crash, a carjacking. There was such a fine line between happiness and misery: I remembered the night we found out my mom had gone missing. I'd just come back from a birthday party at a friend's house and had been so happy and oblivious. And then everything had changed.

Nancy Weller announced it was five minutes until the new year. The crowd cheered. Nancy was giving a speech but I couldn't listen to a word; my mind was filled with scenarios of airplane disasters. My heart began to pound and I felt like my chest might explode. Even though our dad had been sick with heart disease long before his heart attack, I still hadn't been prepared for losing him. What if Sam and I were somehow cursed with bad things happening to us? What if I was going to lose Colin now, too?

Someone touched my shoulder.

Colin.

"What's wrong?" he asked me. "You look upset."

"I thought—"

"My plane got delayed in Boston. I just got in," he said.

I hugged him as the crowd counted down to midnight. Would I ever be normal, and not worry about losing the people I loved?

I *loved*. Did I just think that? Did I *love* him?

"THREE...TWO...ONE..." The crowd boomed and cheered; trumpets blared and confetti fell down around us.

And then Colin kissed me. I closed my eyes and thought: *I love him*.

Seven

On Friday morning Sam drove me to school, and as we passed the canal I spotted a woman and three men dressed in black, standing at the canal's edge, staring down at the dry bed. One man wore a suit and sunglasses.

Sam paused at the stoplight.

"Can we get water in this thing, please? Get me water in this thing!" the man in sunglasses shouted at the others.

"They're here," Sam said, raising her eyebrows.

Mackenzie, Colin, and I went to the diner right after school. A sign made out of a paper place mat had been taped to the door:

Closed for important business (GRIFFIN ON THE GO TV SHOW!!!!) Sorry for the inconvenience!! Will reopen on Jan. 8th. THANKS!!!!

—Wilda

We stepped inside. Several burly men were rearranging the furniture, moving tables, and even hoisting around the decorations. Wilda winced as they picked up a six-foot ceramic red rose. "Careful!" she shouted. "That's valuable!" A man in leather pants took readings with a light meter, and another man with tattoos on his arms moved sound equipment on rolling carts around the diner.

Most of the tables had been pushed to one side of the room, and the counter had been topped with a fancy tablecloth and a vase of fresh flowers. I caught a glimpse of Wilda's cat, Betty, crouching under a booth, then making a mad dash for the kitchen. The man in sunglasses who I'd seen by the canal that morning paced around.

Wilda caught sight of us. "There you are! I want you to meet Blaine MacPhail, the director. Blaine, this is Sophie Scott and her friends Colin Wright and Mackenzie Allen."

"Are you the camera-shy girl?" Blaine asked.

I nodded awkwardly. "Yeah. That's me."

"Nice recipe. We're excited to use it."

Griffin stepped through the doors from the kitchen. I recognized him from the photo—he was even better-looking in person. He was tall with broad shoulders, thick brown hair, and bright green eyes; he was startlingly handsome. He smiled when he saw us, and there was something magnetic about him. Mackenzie sighed.

"And who do we have here?" he asked Wilda, putting his arm lightly around her shoulders.

Wilda blushed, and introduced us. Griffin shook Colin's hand firmly, and kissed Mackenzie and me on both cheeks.

"The recipe you and Wilda devised is just wonderful," Griffin said to me. "And no one told me this town was full of such beautiful women."

Wilda, Mackenzie, and I giggled, embarrassed.

"Sesame seeds—it's ingenious. And they're so perfectly fluffy," he said.

"Thanks." I shrugged.

"I'd like to invite you to dinner tonight—a small casual affair here at the diner—whenever we visit a new town I like to show my appreciation for your generosity in hosting us by preparing a dinner in the winner's honor. Tonight, say, eight o'clock? You're all invited," Griffin said.

"Is it okay—can I ask my sister, too?" I asked.

"Of course! The more the merrier."

He was interrupted by a tall woman smoking a cigarette who spoke to him in French. He said something back to her, and then turned to Wilda. "Wilda, my darling, Yvonne needs you in makeup."

"Oh—okay," Wilda said, looking nervous, and followed Yvonne upstairs.

A very tall, muscular, middle-aged woman with black-rimmed glasses—the woman I'd seen at the canal that morning—came up to Griffin. "We need to go over the script for tomorrow," she told him.

"Krista, let me introduce you to Sophie Scott, the co-creator of the recipe—Sophie, Colin, Mackenzie, this is Krista Drang, the show producer and its wonderful food writer. She writes all the lovely words that come out of my mouth."

"A pleasure," Krista said, and shook our hands. "Griffin, can I speak with you privately?"

"Please excuse me," he told us. "See you tonight!"

Colin, Mackenzie, and I moved to a corner and watched the diner being transformed.

"I wonder where all these people are staying?" Mackenzie asked as we watched the crew buzz around the restaurant.

The guy in the leather pants overheard her. "Ye Olde Venice Inn. We booked the whole place." He put down his light meter and stretched out his hand. "I'm Tim Nubbins. Everyone calls me Nubbs. Nice to meet you." He was thin, with bright red hair and three silver earrings in his left ear. We shook hands and introduced ourselves.

"How many people are on the crew?" Colin asked.

"Ten on the location crew, eleven total including the talent. There's me, I'm the DP, and we've got Bob and Mick on cameras, Nikki Glimcher the food stylist, Yvonne Zamora does makeup and wardrobe; there's Topher Uggman, the gaffer; Jimmy Sniffen, the grip; and Fitz Pickwick, the PA." He pointed at them as he said their names.

He saw the looks of confusion on our faces.

"DP's 'director of photography'—I make sure it all films well; a gaffer does the lighting, the grip is the brawn on the set, and Fitz is the production assistant— he helps out everybody." He ran through the explanations quickly; clearly he'd been asked this before.

"Springwater! Where's my springwater?!" Blaine called out. Fitz ran up beside him with a glass. "You know I don't drink tap," Blaine scolded him. "Who knows what's in tap water in these parts of the country? This is where they dump nuclear waste—these rural towns in America that nobody cares about." Fitz scurried out the door.

"That's a lovely sentiment," I said.

Nubbs folded his arms. "Blaine's from New York City," he said, as if that would explain everything. "I'm an Iowa boy myself. Grew up in Davenport. It's good to be back in the Midwest. We just got done shooting in Nepal—you know what it's like trying to get good lighting on a yak?"

We shook our heads.

"It's not easy. Hey, do you know where a guy can get a beer around here? How about a movie theater?"

"There's a bar called Muther's," Colin said, and gave him directions. "And there's a cineplex at the mall, but a new artsy theater just opened up—it's in our friend's barn." He told him how to get to Fred's house.

"Thanks," Nubbs said.

"What's that woman doing?" I asked, pointing to the food stylist, Nikki Glimcher, who appeared to be shaving a matzo ball with a tiny razor.

"Nikki—watcha doin'?" Nubbs called out.

"Just getting them into ball shape," she said. She put down her razor, stepped back, nodded at her work, and then started polishing silverware.

Griffin paused in his chat with Krista. "Nikki, no—the dumplings aren't supposed to look perfect. That's their beauty—they're *natural*. Make them look natural."

Nikki gave him a dirty look.

A little while later, Wilda came downstairs. At least she resembled someone who had once been Wilda: her

normally bouffant hairdo had been completely deflated;
it was stick straight. She looked about four inches
shorter without the puffy hair. She wore a white dress
with a black waistband, and copious amounts of sparkly
dark eye shadow rimmed her eyes.

"Yvonne Zamora gave me a makeover!" she said. "Do
I look sophisticated?"

"Definitely," I said.

"You should see all the products she has—a whole
suitcase of them," Wilda said.

I felt a pang of longing to be on the show so that I
could try out Yvonne's products. "Do you think she
would give me a makeover even if I'm not on camera?"

"I'll ask her," Wilda said.

Colin smiled. He'd been surprisingly understanding
when I'd told him about my so-called phobia. Apparently
he also understood my love for beauty products.

Mackenzie, a fellow devoted makeup lover, said,
"Can you ask for me too?"

"Of course." Wilda nodded. "Not that you girls need
makeovers."

Griffin paused in conversation with Krista and Blaine,
eyed Wilda, and shook his head. "Where's Yvonne?"

She appeared in the hallway with a cigarette.

"Yvonne! What did you do? Please take some of that
makeup off. She's not on a Paris runway," Griffin said.

Yvonne huffed back up the stairs and waved for
Wilda to follow.

Griffin returned to Krista and Blaine; the three of
them sat at a table near us. "Now what's this place you

want to film called again?" Griffin asked Krista.

"Chocosub," she said.

Colin grinned. "I remember those—those old candy bars?" he whispered. "They were really popular in the midnineties for a couple years."

"I know—I used to love them," Mackenzie said. "They were addictive. And they had like, lots of vitamins and minerals, too, didn't they? They were sort of the first energy bar. But they tasted good."

"Must've been a local thing because I never heard of them," I said. "Sort of a weird name for a candy bar."

"They were shaped like a submarine and were supposed to last forever," Mackenzie said.

I shrugged. "I guess we didn't get them in Cleveland."

"Speaking of chocolate, get me a Slim-Fast bar!" Blaine barked at Fitz. Fitz bumped into us as he scuttled out the door. The cameramen started moving equipment in our direction.

"Let's get out of here," Colin said, and the three of us left the diner. I did a double take when we stepped outside. A line was forming alongside the restaurant. Henry, who worked in Venice High's cafeteria, was first.

"I think the diner's going to be closed for over a week," I told Henry. "There's no point in waiting."

"Oh, I'm not here for food," Henry said matter-of-factly.

"What are you here for?" I asked.

"Griffin's autograph!" he said as if it was a no-brainer. "Did you see him? Tell me everything."

"He's really good-looking," Mackenzie said. "He looks even better in person."

"Really? Did he talk to you?"

We nodded.

"What did he say?" Henry asked eagerly.

"Um...I don't know, a bunch of stuff. We're going back there tonight for dinner," I said.

"You're kidding me. Dinner? Can I come? Please?"

"I don't think it's up to us," I said, wishing I hadn't mentioned it. "Maybe you can ask Wilda?"

He nodded and a look of pure determination took over his face. "See you tonight," he said.

"I had no idea Griffin was this famous," Colin said as we walked past the crowd, which was stretching halfway down the block.

We saw Bea Sellers, president of the Rose Society, clutching the *Rose Petal Cookbook* she'd self-published. Noelle McBride, the most popular and most annoying girl in Venice, was farther down the line; her friends Tara, Claire, and Lacey were beside her, fixing her hair. "I have to get on TV," she told them. "I have to!" Pete Teagarden stood behind her, clutching something resembling a foil-wrapped fireplace log.

We walked Mackenzie to her car. "See you tonight," I said, and hugged her good-bye. Colin and I walked the rest of the way home.

"Do you think Griffin's that handsome?" Colin asked me.

"I have all the beefcake I need right here," I said, touching his arm.

He laughed. "I don't think that word exactly suits me."

* * *

Everyone dressed up for dinner that night: Sam wore wool pants and a silk blouse that used to be our mom's, and Mackenzie and I wore black dresses. Colin met us at our house in a crisp white shirt and dark blazer. He looked so handsome I was tempted to go the way of the chickens. I had to remind myself that we were taking things slow.

We ran into Gus outside the diner; he wore his favorite plaid suit, a relic from the seventies.

"Have you met Griffin yet?" Gus asked us.

We nodded.

"What do you think?"

"He's a hunkola and a half," Mackenzie said. "My mom is jealous I got to come tonight—she gave me three of his cookbooks to get autographed."

She showed us her mom's copies of *Around the World in 80 Meals; Griffin on the Go from Paris, Texas, to Paris, France;* and *Chicken with Griffin.*

We stepped inside the diner; I hardly recognized it. The lights had been dimmed, and candles and fresh flowers decorated one long table. The Petal had been transformed from a country diner into an elegant restaurant.

Griffin was cooking in the back with Fitz. People milled about, drinking wine—I said hello to Nancy Weller, the mayor; Wilda (with her new hair, but less makeup), Bea Sellers, and Henry, who'd successfully garnered an invite.

Gus blinked at Wilda.

"Do you like it?" she asked him, touching her hair and smoothing her dress. "It's my new look."

"I didn't even recognize you," he said.

"Well—Yvonne thought my hair was too big." She looked down at herself. "You don't like it?"

Gus shrugged.

"You look great," I assured her.

Nancy shook my hand. "I have to thank you—I don't think I've ever seen Venice buzzing so much. Your recipe has done a wonderful thing for our town," she said to Wilda and me. "I just hope our little hamlet can withstand the publicity." Nancy laughed.

"It seems like a strange force has taken over the town already—I had fourteen people call the shop tonight asking for Griffin's cookbooks and memorabilia," Colin said.

The kitchen doors flung open and Fitz emerged with a platter of hors d'oeuvres.

"First course!" Griffin shouted from behind him. "What we have here is a lightly fried slice of apple with toasted goat cheese and fried onion frizzles on top."

"Frizzles?" Gus asked.

"Deep-fried onions, sliced perfectly thin," Griffin explained.

Fitz passed them around, along with napkins imprinted with *Griffin on the Go*, Sundays 8 P.M. EST.

Wilda ate one and moaned in ecstasy. "Holy mackerel, this is good."

"It's pure artistry," Henry agreed. "He's the da Vinci of food."

"He has the gift," Bea said solemnly.

Gus shrugged. "Tastes like an onion ring with apple and cheese."

Fitz passed out another tray of them. Henry took three.

"Just wait till you see what I have for dessert for you, Wilda—it's your favorite," Griffin said as he and Fitz returned to the kitchen.

"Pie?" Wilda asked hopefully.

Griffin smiled slyly. "Please, everyone, take your seats. Wilda, why don't you sit next to me." He pointed to a chair beside the head of the table. He disappeared behind the kitchen doors.

There was a rush of people angling to sit closest to Griffin; Gus got left behind at the other end of the table. "Henry, can I switch with you?" he asked, so he could sit next to Wilda.

"No way, buddy," Henry said, firmly planted in his seat.

Fitz soon returned with the first course of the meal. "Primo," Griffin shouted behind him. "Mixed greens with truffle-oil dressing."

Wilda gasped. "I've read about truffle oil."

"What the hell's truffle oil?" Gus asked.

"I brought it here myself from Provence," Griffin said. "I have a friend in Arles, Marcel, who has his own truffle-hunting pig." He launched into a story about truffle-hunting pigs; I stopped listening and started eating. The salad was delicious—it put sesame matzo balls to shame—and right after we'd finished it, Fitz brought out the main course.

"Chicken on the throne," Griffin announced. It was a perfectly browned chicken served upright in a roasting pan, with its legs and wings sticking out as if it was sitting on a chair.

"I took off the top of a can of beer—plain old Budweiser in this case, from your local Kroger's—stuck the beer can inside the chicken's cavity, and cooked it with the can of beer inside it. We did a show in Savannah years ago—that's where I picked up this recipe. You'll see it results in an unusually juicy bird."

I could see the bottom of the beer can sticking out below the chicken's bottom.

"Isn't that in *Around the World in 80 Meals*?" Henry asked. He nodded knowingly.

"It is," Griffin said, and looked pleased.

"I think I've had this before," Gus said. "I was told it was called beer-in-the-butt chicken."

"*Gus,*" Wilda admonished from across the table. "Please."

"It was," Gus said, and shrugged.

Whatever it was called, the chicken was incredibly tender, juicy, and scrumptious. I ate everything on my plate, including the side dishes of rosemary potatoes and sautéed spinach, and Fitz brought out another chicken, for second helpings.

Griffin had also traveled with his own wine, which he served us freely—Wilda looked a little nervous as he poured it to Colin, Mackenzie, and me, but he assured her, "It will complement the meal. It's just a glass." Mackenzie and I grinned at each other. I couldn't remember when I'd last eaten this much—at Thanksgiving, I'd hardly touched a bite, since I was so thrilled about my first kiss with Colin. I smiled at him, thinking about it.

When she'd finished her chicken, Wilda said, "Griffin,

I think this is the most wonderful meal I've ever eaten. Thank you so much."

"Yes—thank you, Griffin," Nancy said.

"You're an artiste," Bea said.

"To Griffin!" Henry said, raising his glass, and soon everyone joined him and gave Griffin a standing ovation. Gus stood up, but clapped halfheartedly.

"Stop," Griffin said. "Really." Then he reached across the table for Wilda's hand, and then mine, and kissed them. "Anything for the women who invented the Petal Diner dumpling." Colin looked slightly annoyed.

"Now, if you'll excuse me, I'm going to prepare the dessert," Griffin said.

He returned to the kitchen. As the doors swung open, I caught a glimpse of Fitz crouched on a stool in there, eating by himself. Griffin said something to him, and Fitz put down his plate, came into the dining room, and cleared our dinner dishes. Clearly, being a PA sucked.

Wilda looked at me. "I can't take all this credit for the dumplings—it's Sophie and Sam's mom's recipe and—"

"Take the credit, Wilda," I said. "Really, your additions made it what it is." *Which is nothing like a matzo ball, thankfully, for the sake of our identities.* Sam nodded vehemently.

"Are you sure you don't want your mom to have some credit, though?" Colin asked quietly. "They could mention her name on the show or something. I think that would be important to me, if it was my mom."

"No," I said a little too sharply. "I mean—I just—she wouldn't want it, really."

Colin nodded.

I stared at my napkin. I wished I could just tell him the truth.

A few minutes later, Griffin brought out the dessert himself. It was a huge, bubbly, sweet-smelling pie. Wilda's eyes widened.

"Fruits of the forest," Griffin said. "I picked the recipe up ten years ago in Appalachia. It's filled with raspberries, strawberries, blueberries, blackberries, rhubarb, peaches, and apples."

Wilda let out a yelp of appreciation.

He served us slices, and Fitz went around the table dolloping homemade vanilla ice cream on top.

I didn't want to say it in front of Wilda because I loved her pie, too, but this was the best pie I'd ever eaten. It was perfectly sweetened—slightly tart and not too sugary—and the crust was moist and flaky.

"Where did you get these berries in the middle of winter? Are they frozen? Canned?" Wilda asked.

"I have my secret ways," Griffin said. He grinned.

Fitz poured coffee as we finished the pie, and people relaxed in their chairs, chatting. Henry loosened his belt.

"We've got a big day tomorrow," Wilda told me. "We need to be on the set at six A.M."

"Six A.M.?" I shuddered. "Really?"

Wilda nodded. "I'm sorry—I was supposed to tell you earlier. Is that a problem?"

"Um—" I didn't know being an offscreen adviser involved waking up at five-thirty in the morning.

"Please come," Wilda said. "The dumplings need you."

"I will." I glanced at my watch; it was almost eleven o'clock. "We should probably get going, then."

"I've got a big workday tomorrow, too," Gus said, pushing his chair out from the table.

Sam raised her eyebrows—their only case at the moment was updating the "lost alumni" files for the Venice High School database, which they didn't need to work on on a Saturday.

"I'm a detective," Gus explained to Griffin. "A PI."

"That must be fascinating," Griffin said, not sounding very fascinated. "Well, all—thank you for coming, and for having me in your wonderful town."

Everyone stood up and thanked him for the fabulous meal. I wanted to thank Fitz, too, but he was nowhere to be seen. Mackenzie and Henry asked Griffin to sign their cookbooks, which he did happily, and then we said good-bye.

Gus waited to say good night to Wilda, but she was absorbed in conversation with Griffin. He tapped her shoulder. "Good night," he said.

"Oh Gus, I'm sorry, I didn't get to—"

Griffin interrupted her. "Fitz is packing up the ingredients—I need to show you the flour I used for the crust," he said, leading her by the arm into the kitchen before she could even finish her sentence.

Gus grimaced and walked out with me; the others were waiting in front of the diner.

"He's a really good cook," Sam said as we shut the door behind us.

Gus buttoned his coat. "I guess."

"Did you guys notice how he was flirting with Wilda?" Mackenzie asked. "He must really like her a whole—"

Gus looked away and said, "I need to get going. Good night," and turned and walked down the street.

"I shouldn't have said that—I forgot—" Mackenzie said.

"Poor Gus," Sam said. "But Wilda's not going to go for Griffin."

"Of course she wouldn't," I said.

The next morning I stumbled in the predawn darkness to the Petal. The diner was already hopping: Fitz arranged doughnuts on a tray and brewed coffee; Wilda sat on a stool in her bathrobe while Yvonne brushed powder on her face with one hand and smoked a cigarette with the other. Nikki sorted through a pile of sesame seeds with a tweezer, picking out the most film-worthy ones; Topher, the gaffer, adjusted the lights to get the best view of the sesames. Griffin examined the dress Wilda was supposed to wear that day and told Yvonne she had to come up with another one. And Nubbs gave directions to the cameramen.

"We're shooting a B roll this morning," Nubbs explained to me.

"A what?" I asked, munching on a doughnut and hoping the coffee would soon kick in.

"A beauty roll—shots of the food looking pretty. Then we're going to do some location shots of Wilda and Griff for the intro montage. We're going to Miller Farm and Centerville Organics later on."

"No cooking today?" I asked.

"Not yet." He glanced at me. "Cooking scenes won't start till Wednesday. You know, I met someone else once who had a phobia like you. She went berserk if anyone pointed a camera at her. One time she had such a severe panic attack she had to go to the hospital."

I nodded. "It's a tough condition, a phobia. I guess I just have to live with it."

"Do you know what caused it? Your parents make too many home videos of you or something?" he asked.

"I think they did."

"Well, maybe you'll get over it when you get older."

"I hope so."

Krista and Griffin sat at a table nearby and went over the script. Krista was really pretty, except for skin that had been tanned a bit too much and bleached hair that was the texture of lamb's wool. "How did the dinner go last night?" she asked him.

Griffin said, "Oh, good, good—Wilda, you know, is a lovely, lovely woman. We'll definitely have on-screen chemistry—I think this will be one of the best episodes yet."

"You say that every time."

"This time I—"

I couldn't hear the rest because Blaine started shouting at Fitz: "Where are the bagels?! I told you to get bagels. You know I don't eat any fat. Get those dough-nuts away from me!"

Fitz scurried out the door.

Nikki started painting a clear glaze on an array of

eggs. Topher, the gaffer, came over to where Nubbs and I were sitting. He had long brown hair in a ponytail, and wore a tie-dyed T-shirt. He gazed at Nikki like a lovesick puppy.

"Nikki's got a real gift, you know," Topher told us. "She's so talented. In Belarus, she made that mutton stew—looked like a pile of crap, but in her hands it became the most beautiful thing."

"She's pretty good," Nubbs agreed. "Hey—can you reposition that arc light? There are huge shadows behind the eggs."

Topher moved the lights around, and Nubbs told me, "That boy's got eyes for Nikki."

"I noticed," I said.

"It gets to be a pretty tight-knit group, being on the crew...people fall for each other all the time. Especially on location. Griffin and Yvonne used to be a couple."

Blaine, still in his sunglasses, saw us talking. "Back to work, this isn't a kaffeeklatsch," he said, and stared at me. He folded his arms. "Shy girl. How's that doughnut? Guess you can afford those fat grams at your age."

I nodded shyly.

He took off his sunglasses. "You know I used to be shy myself. But I got over it." He patted me on the shoulder, and sat down with Griffin and Krista.

I decided to go talk to Fitz, who'd returned with a package of Lender's bagels and was spreading one with fat-free cream cheese. He had a spot of dried blood on his face where he'd cut himself shaving, and a speck of toilet paper stuck to it.

"Hey, I wanted to thank you for dinner last night. It was really delicious—I had a great time. Griffin's such a good cook."

"Yeah, right." He sniffed.

"I know you worked really hard—I wanted you to know I appreciated it."

"Yeah. Sure. Worked hard. Cooked the whole damn meal," he muttered.

"Didn't Griffin help?"

He laughed. "People keep thinking that." He stabbed the knife into the tub of cream cheese, where it stood upright. His face was red.

"All righty," I said, and backed away. He looked like he was about to go postal.

Nubbs was giving directions to Topher and Jimmy Sniffen, the grip. I sat down by myself and began to wonder why I was there—it didn't seem like I had any place in the show, except as an officially sanctioned observer. I continued to watch the commotion—Nikki seemed to be performing surgery on a stalk of celery, and Yvonne attacked Wilda's hair with a straightening iron while Griffin complained she was making it too flat. Blaine briefed Wilda on the locations they'd be shooting later that afternoon.

I asked Krista, "Is there anything for me to do?"

She stared at me. "Well—not really. You're positive you don't want to be on camera?"

"I'm sure," I said.

She shook her head. "I'm sorry, but we really don't have anything for you to do right now."

"Okay," I said. "I think I'm going to take off, then."

"I'll let you know if we think of something," Krista said. I tried to get Wilda's attention to say good-bye, but she couldn't hear me amid Blaine, Griffin, and Yvonne arguing over what outfit she should wear that day.

I gave up, slipped out the door, and walked home. It was eight-thirty, and Sam was still asleep. I got back into bed and within minutes I was asleep, too.

When I woke up two hours later, Sam was in the kitchen reading the newspaper. "What happened? Why aren't you at the diner?" she asked me.

"I didn't have anything to do there." I shrugged. "It's pretty boring being off camera. I think I'm just going to let Wilda take over—I mean it's not like it's really Mommy's recipe, anyway."

"That's for sure," Sam said, raising her eyebrows. "What was it like on the set?"

I rolled my eyes. "It's kind of nuts. The director kept yelling at Fitz, the gaffer likes the food stylist, and the makeup lady used to go out with Griffin."

"Sounds more like a soap opera than a food show," Sam said.

"It is." I ate a spoonful of Cheerios, and then the phone started ringing.

It was Henry. "Do you know where they're filming to-day?" he asked. "I heard they might be going to the poultry farm, or to that organic market in Centerville. I want to go watch. I'm hoping I can get on as an extra, in the background with the poultry."

"Someone mentioned something about Centerville

Organics and Miller Farm, but I don't know when they're going there." I explained what had happened that morning, and how I didn't plan on going back.

"You need to get over that camera fear, young lady," Henry said. "You're missing the opportunity of a lifetime." He pressed me for more information about Griffin's schedule, then finally gave up.

As soon as I'd said good-bye to Henry, the phone rang again. It was Bea Sellers. "I was hoping you'd know where they're filming," she said.

"I just got off the phone with Henry—he wanted to know the same thing." I repeated everything I'd told him.

After that I got calls from Ethel Gooseberry, who drove the schoolbus, Celeste, our landlady, Mrs. Philbert, the principal of Venice High, and from Chester, all wanting information about Griffin, the show, and what sites they planned to film. Apparently I'd been elected the *Griffin on the Go* town liaison. Sam and I finally turned the ringer off so we could have a little peace, but a few hours later there was a knock on the door.

It was Pete Teagarden, my ex-crush (number three). He was carrying the same huge foil-wrapped fireplace log that he'd been holding when he was in line outside the diner.

"I need to ask you something," he said. "It's really important."

"What is it?"

"I need you to give something to Griffin for me."

"Why don't you just give it to him yourself?" I explained once more that I wasn't going to have much of a role with the show. "And anyway, I think they're out filming on location—I'm not even sure where they are."

"No, they're back at the diner now. I just walked by and saw them in there. Look, I need your help—I can't go there by myself—I tried and I couldn't get in to talk to Griffin. I need an endorsement from you. You have an in with them." He gripped his log closer.

I stared at it, and it began to dawn on me what it was. During our unfortunate date last October, he'd told me he might want to be a chef someday, and he'd described his visionary creation to me: "I'm going to take an enchilada, wrap it in a burrito, stick it in a taco, and serve it inside a tostada," he'd said. "I'm going to call it 'The Conundrum.'"

"Is that—?" I asked, pointing at the log and peering at it sideways.

He grinned. "The Conundrum."

I nodded.

"Can you at least come with me to the diner? If we go right now, you can introduce me to him," he said.

I paused. During our date he'd tried to kiss me with his mouth open so wide that he'd looked like a crazed Muppet—I could practically see his tonsils. He looked a lot more composed now, but still desperate, standing there.

"Please," he pleaded, his entire football-player body sagging. *"Please."*

I sighed. "Fine. I'll introduce you, but you can explain what it is yourself." I put on my coat and Pete and I walked to the diner.

"Thanks," he said. "I really, really, *really* appreciate it."

When we reached the Petal, Griffin was sitting at a table with Krista, who was taking notes on a legal pad.

"I refuse to have Wilda dressed in that black frock Yvonne picked—it doesn't do justice to her curves—" Griffin was saying.

They looked up as Pete and I headed toward them.

"Hi," I said. "I'm sorry to interrupt—I just wanted to introduce you to a friend of mine."

Pete Teagarden flashed a Cheshire cat grin. He opened the aluminum-foil-wrapped Conundrum, and explained what it was.

Griffin stared at it. "Interesting."

Krista looked perplexed.

"Do you want to try it?" Pete asked.

"Sure. Fork, please." Griffin waved his hand, and Fitz appeared with a fork a few seconds later. He almost looked like he wanted to stab Griffin with it.

Griffin was completely oblivious. He took a bite. "Not bad, actually. It could use a touch more cumin, I think, and fresh cilantro." He chewed meditatively, and put down his fork. "It's really quite good." He patted Pete on the shoulder. "Good job."

Pete looked like he'd just won the lottery. "Really? Do you mean it?"

"Of course I do!" Griffin said. "Krista, try it."

She looked wary, but took a bite. She paused. "It's very unique. Good luck with it." She turned to Griffin. "Fine. Yvonne's not going to be happy, but I'll tell her you want to nix the dress…"

"I can't believe he likes it," Pete told me as we

walked away. "He likes my Conundrum." His eyes had a dreamy, faraway look.

"Hey—can I taste it?" I asked.

We took a fork from the catering table and I tried it. It tasted like canned refried beans mixed with sawdust and soggy corn meal. It was gross. Griffin and Krista had been extremely nice.

"It's good," I lied, figuring there was no point in stomping on his dreams.

"I wish I'd known about the contest for the show—I hadn't heard of it before Wilda won," he said. He gingerly wrapped up the remains of the Conundrum in foil. "I would've submitted my recipe."

"Well, maybe next year they'll have the contest again," I said.

"Maybe," he said. "I really need to get on this show."

We left the diner. A line had formed outside again. There were a lot of people I didn't recognize, who'd probably come from other towns. At the end of the line I saw someone familiar: Officer Alby, who was clutching a copy of *Griffin Is Grillin'*. I tried to duck behind Pete so Alby wouldn't see me—Difriggio had said to avoid him—but he scrutinized me as I walked by.

"Why is he looking at you like that?" Pete asked me.

"I don't know." My voice was faint. I shrugged and looked away. Alby's intense stare made a chill run down my spine.

That night, Sam, Josh, and Colin and I went to the movies at Fred's. He showed the food film *Big Night* in honor of *Griffin on the Go* coming to town.

"I'm glad you decided not to be on the show—when I walked by the diner tonight it looked like they were still filming," Colin said. "I'd never get to see you."

I nodded. "I know—I'm glad I'm not, too."

Josh, of course, knew why I didn't want to be on TV; he smiled to himself. "A snowstorm is supposed to hit tonight," he told us, changing the subject. "We should all go sledding tomorrow."

We made plans for the next day, and when I got home there was a message from Wilda.

I called her back. "We just finished shooting," she said. It was eleven-thirty at night. "And we have to start again at six A.M. tomorrow. Lord, I'm beat. I can see why you don't want to do it."

"I hope you don't mind."

"I understand," she said. "You must've been so bored. And I had no idea a food show was so much work. I didn't know they'd have a script with lines for me to memorize and everything. And all the time with makeup and wardrobe—it's a food show, and I hardly even got a chance to eat! I'm making myself a burger." I could hear the pan sizzling. "We're going to scout out some more locations tomorrow. Hopefully it won't be as long a day."

I told her about the forecast for snow.

"Maybe they'll give us a day off, then," Wilda said. "I sure hope so. Well—I'll call you tomorrow." I wished her good night.

* * *

The snowstorm hit Venice later that night, and when we woke up the next morning there was over two feet on the ground. The whole town resembled a magical fairyland, with tree limbs encased in a lattice of white ice, and a white river where the street had once been. Everything was quiet.

That afternoon, after the roads were plowed, Josh met us at Colin's to go sledding. I felt like we were little kids, tramping through the snow and making angels. At one point Colin and I sneaked a kiss behind a tree. I thought we were hidden from view until a snowball landed in the middle of my back, thrown by Sam. She'd become comfortable with the idea of us being together, so long as we took it slow—and apparently as long as she didn't have to actually see us kiss.

I threw a snowball back at her. She ran away. Josh got into the fray and threw one at me; Colin threw one at him, and before we knew it, we were in a huge snowball fight. We threw them at one another all the way home, until we reached Colin's shop. We built a snowman in his front yard, and then headed inside for hot chocolate and marshmallows. We ordered pizza for dinner.

"Lorna Scrabble time?" Sam asked when we finished eating. We always played Lorna Scrabble, a version of the game our mom had made up. The only rule was that you had to make up fictional words from the letters you picked, then invent a plausible definition for each word; if you used a real word, you lost the game. "Or Boggle?"

Josh walked over to the toy section of Colin's store. "How about another game for a change?" He looked through the aging boxes on the shelves. "You three have a distinct advantage with word games, so I think I need something different if I'll ever catch up to your winning level. All right, let's see...what do we have here." Josh picked up a few boxes. "Hungry Hungry Hippos? No. How about Pictionary?"

"I love Pictionary," I said.

"Me, too," Sam said.

We played with Josh and Sam on one team, and Colin and me on another. It went pretty well until I got the term *grocery bag*. I drew the most obvious thing: a plastic bag hanging off a tree limb, as they often did on our Queens block. I'd woken up many a morning in our old house and stared at the plastic Food Dynasty bags on the tree out my window.

"A leaf? Bird feeder? Lantern!" Colin shouted helplessly.

I circled the bag in the tree again and again, as if that would make him get the point.

Then the time was up. "It's a grocery bag!" I told him.

Colin looked bewildered. "Why would a grocery bag be in a tree?"

I sighed. "Because that's where they get stuck sometimes, from the wind."

He looked at me like I was crazy.

Sam decided to change the subject. "Next word," she said. We played several more rounds until there was a knock on the door. It was almost ten o'clock at night.

"Maybe it's that food stylist, Nikki Glimcher," Colin

said, shrugging. "She left three messages today asking if I had an extra silver knife for the shoot."

But when he opened the door, Gus was standing there.

Gus's face was solemn. "Wilda ran off with Griffin," he said.

Eight

We invited Gus inside. He didn't even take his coat off; he just slumped on the couch and fiddled with his hands. "Wilda's suitcase is missing, and so is Griffin's. They left a note."

"What?" My mouth dropped open.

Gus took a piece of paper out of his pocket. "I stopped by Wilda's tonight—I went up to her apartment and knocked on the door, but there was no answer. I looked inside but she wasn't there, so I went down to the diner. The crew had left and a note was pinned to the white tablecloth on the counter."

He showed it to us. "It's not in Wilda's handwriting. The buffoon wrote it," he said.

> Food Folk—
> We're off on a romantic excursion—be back when we're back.
> Toujours,
> GG and WH

"This can't be for real," I said.

"I called Blaine and Krista and they said the shooting for the day had wrapped at seven o'clock—three hours ago. No one has seen them since. Blaine and Krista are both worried—apparently Griffin has done this before. In Italy, he disappeared with a woman for three days, Blaine said. In Greece, two days. In Uzbekistan, he went off with a woman and a donkey and didn't come back for a week. Blaine checked in Griffin's room at the hotel and his suitcase is missing."

I shook my head. "Wilda wouldn't do that," I said. "Leave Betty? And you?" I realized after I said it that I should've mentioned Gus before the cat. "She wouldn't have left you for Griffin." That's what I had meant to say. "And I talked to her last night—she didn't mention anything about leaving, or being interested in Griffin, or anything."

Gus still looked glum. "I think it's my fault. She didn't like it that I was embarrassed that people knew about us."

"That's not true," I said, although I knew it was.

Gus shrugged.

"She'd never run off like that," Sam said. "When she went to L.A. she left us three pages of notes on how to take care of Betty."

"I didn't see Betty in the apartment or the diner," Gus said. "Maybe they took the cat with them."

I held up my hands in disbelief.

"Have you checked all the movie theaters and local restaurants? They could've meant that they were just going out for dinner or something," Josh suggested.

"I thought about that. But then I looked in her apartment and saw that her suitcase was gone, too—you know she had that hideous pink one with the embroidered cat on it? Well it's not there anymore."

Sam said, "I don't know. I'm with Sophie. It just doesn't sound like Wilda to run off without telling anyone."

"You never know what goes on in people's heads," Gus said. I wondered if he was thinking of his ex-wife, who'd left him for another man years before.

"Did you see anything missing besides her luggage?" Colin asked.

He shook his head. "No."

"With the snowstorm they couldn't have gotten too far," Josh said. "The roads were pretty slow going when I drove here."

"Good point," Sam said.

"That would be crazy, to drive far in this weather," I said. "Did you check if their cars were gone?"

Gus nodded. "Wilda's is still parked outside the diner. Blaine said Griffin's is missing—it's not in the inn's parking lot."

This wasn't looking good—the clues did point to them having run off together. But I still didn't believe it; I couldn't picture Wilda doing that.

"Well, I'm going to drive around, make sure they didn't get stuck in the snow somewhere between here and Indy—I'm figuring that's where they were headed, if they were thinking of flying out," Gus said. "I just wanted to let you know what had happened. We can look into it more tomorrow."

"We'll come with you," I offered.

"No—it's dangerous driving. I'll go myself. You can help out tomorrow."

I nodded.

"Be careful on the roads," Josh said.

Gus left the shop, got into his car, and drove into the whitened landscape.

It started to snow again that night, and by the next morning another six inches had accumulated. School was canceled, but I couldn't enjoy the break. I was too worried about Wilda. Gus had left us a message late the night before saying that after driving around for hours he hadn't found anything.

Sam and I went to the Petal to see if we could find out any information. News of Wilda and Griffin's disappearance had traveled fast, and the Petal Diner was crowded with people spouting theories as to what might have happened to them.

"I think it's romantic," Fern said; she'd stopped by while walking her dog, Isabel. "To leave with a famous chef and TV star on a romantic vacation! Oh, I bet Griffin flew her off to Paris! Or to Italy! How exciting!" She stared out the window dreamily.

Blaine said, "I'm not one bit surprised that they did it—though I told Griff if he pulled that stunt one more time, I'd fire him."

"You always say that, and you never do," Krista said. "I think we should call Gar."

Blaine flinched.

"Who's Gar?" I asked Nubbs.

"Gar Cabot. He's the executive producer back in New York City—he's everybody's boss, even Blaine's, Krista's, and Griffin's."

"I don't want to bother him with another one of Griffin's petty dalliances," Blaine said.

"Well, I'm going to call him." Krista went into the kitchen with her cell phone.

Blaine followed her. "Wait—let's just give Griff a couple days—he usually comes back after a couple days—"

Yvonne lit a cigarette and examined her fingernails. Nikki rearranged her pile of glazed eggs, looking annoyed. Topher and Jimmy Sniffen played cards with the cameramen. Only Fitz seemed pleased that Griffin was missing; he stood by the coffee urns looking smug. "What do you think happened to them?" I asked as I poured myself a cup of coffee.

"I don't know, but I hope he's dying a slow and painful death. I wish Blaine was with him."

I nodded, and then walked back to Sam.

"The PA is nuts," I whispered. I told her what he'd said.

She eyed him in his black sweatshirt emblazoned with HELL'S KITCHEN. He was slowly tearing a napkin to shreds. "He looks anxious," she said.

"He always looks anxious," I said.

Krista and Blaine returned from the kitchen. "The show must go on," Krista announced.

Blaine rubbed his forehead, looking nervous. "I still think—"

"Gar made no bones about it. We have to find a replacement to shoot the cooking segment," Krista said.

"We can keep the shots of town scenery we have, but we'll redo the montage and the location pieces. Good thing we didn't start the cooking segment yet."

Blaine groaned. "How are we going to reshoot? With who?"

Jimmy Sniffen raised a tattooed arm. "I'd like to do it," he said. "I think I could be a good replacement. We could call it *Sniffen on the Go*," he said.

Blaine laughed. "I don't think so."

"Gar told me I should step in in Griffin's place," Krista said. "That's what I did during the Uzbeki segment, and ratings were good. The problem is we need a recipe and the local talent."

All eyes turned to me. "No," I said. "No way. I'm not going on camera. You know that."

"What about that burrito boy?" Krista asked. "The one who came by the set? What was that dish he had—the Enigma?"

"The Conundrum," I said.

"You want to nix the soup and shoot the burrito boy?" Blaine asked.

"Let's do that," Krista said.

I froze. Pete was going to take Wilda's place, showing the nation (or at least whatever portion of it that watches cable television food shows) how to make a monstrous burrito?

Blaine sighed and turned toward Fitz. "Get the burrito boy on the phone ASAP. Make sure he's not SAG. Does he have an agent?"

"I'll check," Fitz growled.

As I watched Blaine and Krista devise how to strip Pete of all his screen rights, I heard a strange scratching sound. It seemed like it was coming from the door to the basement, near where I was sitting. I stood up and went to the door. I opened it.

Betty stared at me plaintively from the other side. She let out a long, mournful yowl. Everyone stared.

"Who locked the cat in the basement?" I asked. I shook my head, remembering how Zayde had been stuck down there when she'd been lost. I held the door to the basement open. Betty strutted in, then changed her mind. She headed back down the cellar stairs.

"What are you doing?" I said to the cat. "It's freezing down there. Come back!"

Sam gave me a look. "I don't think cats speak English."

"I know that, but—"

"Shut the door, it's colder than Antarctica!" Blaine shouted.

I ran down the stairs after Betty; I didn't want her disappearing into the basement like Zayde had done. Betty trotted into a shadowy corner and sat down behind the water heater. I followed her.

"Oh, gross, there are spiders back here. Yuck." I reached down to pick up Betty. Then I realized what she was sitting on. It was Wilda's suitcase.

"Someone wanted it to *look* like Wilda and Griffin ran off together," Sam told Gus as we sat in his office later that morning.

"And Betty's done the best detective work of any of us so far," I said. "You should hire that cat."

Sam gave me a look. "Please. Let's not go there."

"Maybe Griffin abducted her," Gus suggested. "I never trusted that guy. I don't trust any of these TV people."

"Maybe. Let's put him on our list of suspects," Sam said. She got out a piece of paper and started writing. "Do you know the names of everyone on the crew?" she asked me.

I nodded. I said them out loud as Sam wrote:

Blaine MacPhail, director
Krista Drang, producer and food writer
Tim "Nubbs" Nubbins, DP (director of photography)
Nikki Glimcher, food stylist
Yvonne Zamora, makeup artist
Topher Uggman, gaffer (lighting)
Jimmy Sniffen, grip (the muscles on the set)
Fitz Pickwick, production assistant
Bob and Mick, cameramen

I told them what Nubbs had said to me about Yvonne and Griffin having been a couple, and also what Pete had said about wanting to be on the show. "Doesn't it seem a little too perfect that Pete got to be on it after saying that? Maybe he did something." I shrugged.

"You really think Pete is capable of that?" Sam asked.

"Probably not, but it can't hurt to put him on the list," I said. She wrote his name down.

"So where do we start?" Sam asked.

"We'll interview the crew," Gus said. "See if anyone has an idea what might have happened, or if anyone's noticed something unusual or suspicious. And we need to check alibis during the hours that Wilda and Griffin disappeared."

"We should make up posters, too," I said. "Maybe someone in town or nearby might have spotted them."

I wrote up drafts of two flyers, then gave them to Gus to look over.

Wilda Higgins
5'8"
140 Pounds
Red Hair
Pink Scarf
Pink Coat
Necklace Beaded with Ceramic Black Cats

Griffin Gateaux
6'3"
205 Pounds
Black Italian Suit
Black Coat
Black Shoes
Very Handsome
Brown Hair

Gus approved of Wilda's flyer, but he added a few things to Griffin's description, then handed it back to me.

"'Hair not his own'? 'Ego the size of North America'? 'Noticeable belly'? Gus!" I said.

"He has a belly," Gus maintained. "You just can't tell under those fancy suits."

We left Gus's office and returned to the diner to question the crew. Krista was sitting in a corner with Pete, scribbling away on her notepad. I eyed Pete to see if he looked guilty, but I couldn't tell. I'd never seen him smile so much.

Gus moved a table and four chairs into the stockroom in the back so we could interview the crew in private. Gus asked to speak to Blaine first.

"You're detectives?" Blaine asked with disbelief as he gazed up at the towers of paper towels, napkins, and industrial-size cans of green beans and corn.

"We are," Gus said.

"Licensed?"

Gus took his PI license out of his wallet and showed it to him. Blaine removed his sunglasses and held the license up to the light.

"It's real," Gus said sharply.

"If you say so," Blaine said, and gave it back to him. He glanced at his watch. "I don't know why I'm here. I really don't have time for this. And I'm certain Griffin just took her to some love nest somewhere."

"What about her suitcase being found in the basement?" Gus asked.

He waved his hand. "I know that's a little suspicious, but there must be some explanation for it—maybe Wilda threw it out or something—who knows. Griffin's gone off with a woman he met during filming half a dozen times before." Blaine rolled his eyes. "He's a lothario. Do you know he told me he was actually married once? Can you imagine that man married? Ha!" He let out a false chuckle. "I'll bet you a thousand dollars the two of them are back in three days, flushed from their nonstop romp in bed."

Gus shifted in his seat and scratched his ear. Sam took notes.

"Where were you after you stopped filming last night—after seven P.M.?" Sam asked him.

"I drove back to the hotel with Krista. And Fitz brought me a Slim-Fast bar at eight, and a hot-water bottle at nine—you can check with him. I couldn't have done away with Griffin and Wilda in an hour, could I?" He folded his arms and smiled.

"We're just checking," Gus said.

"Have you noticed anything suspicious on the set— anyone who might want to harm Griffin or Wilda?" I asked.

He laughed. "This is a television show. There's always infighting and rivalries—but no one would do something like *that*." He made a huffing sound and glanced at his watch again. "Are we done yet? I have work to do."

"That's fine for now," Gus said. "We might need to talk to you again later."

"Who knows why," Blaine said. "Look, if you're going

to interview the whole crew, you better do it fast. I need everyone ready to shoot in one hour."

Gus glared at him. "The stars of your show are missing. This is a serious situation."

"They'll be back in three days," Blaine said dismissively. "Now, you've got one hour with my crew."

"Fine," Gus said. Blaine returned to the set.

"We better split up to question the crew," Gus told us. "That's the only way we'll get done in an hour—fifteen minutes or so per suspect." We decided that Gus would talk to Nikki, Topher, Sniffen, and Bob and Mick; Sam and I would interview Krista, Nubbs, Yvonne, and Fitz, and then we'd compare notes.

Gus gave Sam and me use of the stockroom, and we asked Krista to speak with us. She took off her glasses as she sat down. She had dark circles under her eyes; I was surprised she didn't take advantage of having Yvonne on her staff. A good moisturizer and lipstick would do her a world of good.

"Of course they ran off together," she said, rubbing her eyes. "You think he cooks those welcome meals to show his hospitality to the town?" She shook her head. "He just wants to charm the pants off the women who are going to be on the show," she said. "Literally."

"Blaine said Griffin's done that half a dozen times?" Sam asked.

"At least," Krista said. "He gets involved with some woman during every shoot. If not on location, then in the studio."

"We heard he's been involved with Yvonne," I said.

"You heard it? I'm the one who heard it—they were in the room next to mine in the hotel in Provence," she said, shaking her head again. "He had a thing with Nikki, too."

"Really?" Sam asked.

"They snuck off for two days when we were in Belgium."

Krista's alibi corroborated with Blaine's—they'd driven back to the hotel at seven P.M., after the shoot wrapped. "I took an Ambien and hit the pillow," she said. "I was out like a light."

We questioned Yvonne next. She wore a red silk dress and slithered into her chair, crossing her legs. I stared at her knee-high black boots in silent appreciation. She lit a long brown cigarette.

"I think Griffin is off getting plastic surgery somewhere. He was concerned about a small bald spot that was forming on the back of his head," she said in her French accent. "He asked me for a recommendation for a man who performs hair implants. I gave him the name of a doctor in Brazil. Griffin was also interested in having his bags removed." She pointed under her eyes. "He was never good with the skin-treatment regimen I made for him. He never exfoliated. Never!"

"If he went to Brazil for plastic surgery, then where did Wilda go?" Sam asked.

"I do not know." She flicked her cigarette ashes onto the floor—I didn't think Wilda would appreciate that, so I opened a pack of paper cups and handed one to her. Yvonne took it and exhaled a stream of smoke. "I did not like working on Weelda. Everything I did, Griffin did not approve. Maybe she is stuck in a barnyard somewhere. Maybe a sheep ate her," she said. She shrugged. "I am happy it is over."

At least she was honest. And it explained why Wilda wasn't able to arrange a makeover for me.

"I don't think sheep eat people," Sam pointed out.

"Whatever." She waved her hand.

"Well, did you notice anything suspicious on the set?" I asked.

"Certainly. Some of the ladies' clothes from the show wardrobe are missing. I had three pretty dresses—two Chanel and one Diane von Furstenberg. All three are gone. And a prop item—a pink gun—I used for our show in Tombstone."

"*A gun*?" Sam asked.

"Yes," she said excitedly. "I bought it from a woman in Tombstone. It was an antique, with a pink handle. I glued pink feathers on it. We dressed a local woman up as a cowgirl and had a fake gunfight—I did such a nice job." She nodded proudly. "She wore a pink cowboy hat and a sequined skirt...I think Nikki took the gun, and the dresses."

"Nikki?" I asked.

"Yes—I do not trust her."

"Why?"

She puffed her cigarette. "Just a feeling."

"It was a real gun?" Sam asked.

She shrugged. "I think not."

"Um—is it true that you and Griffin used to be a couple?" I asked, trying to say it delicately.

"What does it matter? Yes, we had a moment. One night in Provence we drank too much wine, and so forth. I have no memory of it."

I wondered if she was underplaying how she really felt. Maybe she was trying to sound low-key, but in reality she could have pounced on Griffin in a jealous rage.

Sam asked about her alibi.

She smirked. "I spent the night in Timothy's room."

"Who?" I asked.

"Nubbs," she said.

I raised my eyebrows. Apparently he'd been speaking of himself when he said people on the crew "fall for each other all the time."

We thanked her for talking to us. As Yvonne left, I saw Nubbs waiting by the stockroom door. She shimmied past him and gave him a sultry look. He touched her waist and waved good-bye to her. He was wearing his leather pants again; they squeaked as he sat down.

"Gus told me I should talk to you next," he said. "I'm really sorry about your friend disappearing. I hope they're all right."

He was the first person on the crew to voice real concern for Wilda and Griffin. He actually looked worried about them.

"Thanks," I said. "I hope they're okay, too."

"So you and Yvonne are a couple?" Sam asked him, getting down to business.

He crossed his legs; the pants squeaked again. "Well—sort of—at the moment, yes." He smiled shyly, a little embarrassed at revealing the details of his romantic life.

"At the moment?" Sam asked suspiciously, as if she disapproved of his and Yvonne's uncommitted-couple status. I was afraid she was going to give him a stern lecture on How Babies Are Created. "Yvonne says that you were together during the hours Griffin disappeared?"

He nodded. "We were."

"Do you have a problem with the fact that your lady friend was once involved with Griffin?" she asked.

Nubbs shook his head. "Nah—that didn't mean anything." He took a pack of Big Red gum out of his pocket and offered pieces to us. Sam refused it but I took one.

I liked Nubbs. I thought he seemed more sincere than anyone else on the crew. "What do *you* think happened to Griffin and Wilda?" I asked.

"I have no idea—it would seem in Griffin's character to run off with Wilda, but I just don't know." He shrugged. "I really wish I could help. I keep thinking about whether one of us could've had something to do with it, but I can't picture anyone on this crew doing that."

We asked him a few more questions, but he didn't give us any new information. He glanced at me. "It must be kind of fun being a detective, right? I always wanted to be one—I used to read all those Hardy Boys mysteries—"

"This is the real world, my friend, not the land of Hardy Boys," Sam said curtly. "Thanks for talking to us, not that we learned anything new."

"Sure," Nubbs said, giving her a quizzical look.

I thanked him, and after he'd left I asked Sam, "Why

were you giving him such a hard time? I'm sure he's innocent. He and Yvonne have alibis."

"I don't trust either of them—Yvonne seems sort of
snaky and Nubbs seems, well...I just don't like those
leather pants."

"You can't suspect someone because you don't like
his pants," I said.

"Says who?" she asked, and smiled.

Our last interview was with Fitz. He wore the hood of
his "Hell's Kitchen" sweatshirt over his head as he sat
down in the stockroom.

He launched right into his own soliloquy before we
could even ask him a question. "Honestly, I don't care
what happened to Griffin. Do you think I spent four years
and sixty thousand dollars at NYU film school to deal
with this crap? Last summer I worked on this indie feature, *Squeaky Pigs*—it almost made it to Sundance. I
deserve better than this—treated like a piece of you-
know-what on the set and now I'm being interviewed
about a mysterious disappearance. Great." He said
"mysterious disappearance" mockingly.

Fitz's alibi corroborated with Blaine's. "I wish I could
say I dropped off Blaine's stupid Slim-Fast bar and found
him with bloody hands and Griffin's head rolling around
the room, but that would be perjury." He stared up at the
ceiling. "I wonder if there's some other way I can incrim-
inate him?"

Completely bonkers, I scribbled in my notepad. I
didn't know if he was acting like this just for show, or if
he was really capable of doing something crazy. We
thanked him for talking to us.

"What a wacko," I whispered to Sam after Fitz had left.

"He's cracked," Sam agreed, "but he's got an alibi."

We shut the door to the stockroom and walked past the set—Topher was moving equipment around, Yvonne was combing Pete's hair, and Nikki looked especially stressed as she tried to prepare a photogenic Conundrum—and we reconvened with Gus. We walked back to his office.

Gus told us what he'd learned from his interviews. "Didn't get anything interesting out of Sniffen and the cameramen—they say they were at Muther's when Griffin and Wilda disappeared, which will be easy to check. Nikki's alibi is that she was watching TV in her room, and Topher says he was taking a walk at that time—neither are ironclad to say the least. Nikki also said one of her food-styling knives was stolen—a sharp one. It had a monogram on it of the letter *N*."

"And we've got a missing pink feathered gun on the loose, too," I said. "Although it sounds like it's just a fake prop." We filled him in on our conversations. "Krista told us Griffin and Nikki were a couple once also—do you think Topher's capable of a jealous rage?" Sam asked.

"Topher got a little red around the ears at the mention of Griffin's womanizing—maybe there's a love triangle there," Gus said, looking at his notes.

Our next step, Gus told us, was to investigate Wilda's apartment more closely. He'd done a quick once-over of it the night she disappeared, but we needed to look more thoroughly for clues.

"When do you want to do it?" Sam asked.

"Not when the crew's there. We're technically not supposed to be trespassing on her property. I don't want anyone from the crew—especially the culprit—knowing we're there. Topher told me they're planning on shooting till midnight tonight, though they might go a couple hours over since they're behind schedule," he said.

"So you want to go at two A.M.?" Sam asked.

"Three to be safe," he said.

We made plans to meet at the back door to the diner at three in the morning.

Nine

Colin and Mackenzie came over for dinner that night. "Any news?" Colin asked as I stirred a huge pot of macaroni and cheese.

"Not much." I told them everything we'd learned in the interviews.

"I think Fitz did it," Mackenzie said as she set the table. "He sounds psycho. Maybe he managed to do something during the hours when he wasn't with Blaine."

"Maybe," Sam said.

Mackenzie had brought dessert; when we finished dinner we sat at the kitchen table and devoured a plate of brownies, trying to make sense of what we'd learned. I told them we were going to be breaking into Wilda's apartment later that night.

Sam looked at the clock. "Actually, we should get to bed soon, since we need to wake up at two-thirty."

"I need to get going, too—I'm meeting Fred at his movie theater," Mackenzie said, and her face flushed.

Sam and Colin volunteered to wash the dishes, and Mackenzie and I moved into the living room. "How's everything going with Fred?" I asked her.

"Pretty good, I guess. He actually let me hold the

leash when we took Herman for a walk this afternoon.
That's a good sign, right? He never lets anyone else hold
it."

"Very good sign," I said.

"I better get going." She wished me luck tonight, and
we hugged good-bye.

After Sam and Colin finished up the dishes, Sam let
Colin and me have a few moments alone while we said
good night (so long as the living-room lights were on).

We sat on the couch, and Colin put his arms around
me. "Be careful at Wilda's tonight," he said. "Who knows
if that crazy Fitz is lurking around, or some other nutty
crew member."

"We'll be careful."

He kissed me.

"It's hard when your girlfriend's a detective," he said.
"You just don't get that much time together. I wonder if
Ned had this problem with Nancy Drew."

I blinked. "You just called me your girlfriend." I had
thought the L-word about him just a few days before,
but I still hadn't ever heard him refer to me as his girlfriend.

He looked surprised. "Isn't—aren't you—?"

I grinned. "I am."

Sam's alarm went off at two-thirty, and we got out of
bed and put on our stealth gear: black turtlenecks, black
pants, black jackets, and black wool hats; we looked
more like burglars than detectives. I had butterflies in
my stomach as we drove through Venice in the middle of

the night; it was fun to be up while the whole town slept. Every light was out in the houses we passed. We parked in the back lot of the diner, behind Wilda's abandoned car.

Gus waited for us inside the back entrance, and we all went up to Wilda's apartment together. We looked through her books, closets, shelves of cat figurines, and notes on the refrigerator; in the bedroom I searched the pockets of all her coats. I found lipsticks and mints, spare change and a nail file, but no clues.

I sat on her bedspread, which pictured kittens frolicking with balls of string, while Gus read through her date book in the kitchen and Sam searched the bathroom.

Buried under a pile of books on her nightstand—including the complete cookbooks of Griffin Gateaux—was a small pink cloth-bound book. It looked like a journal.

I opened the cover; I glanced at Wilda's loopy script on the first page without reading it. I shut the book.

I felt strange peeking into her private thoughts. I thought of how I dreaded the idea of someone reading my journal.

"She has even more face creams than you do," Sam said, coming in from the bathroom. "I never even noticed she had wrinkles, and she's got about two dozen wrinkle serums." She stared at the journal in my hands "What's that?"

"Wilda's diary. I feel weird reading it. Do you think we should?"

Gus came into the room and I showed it to him. He didn't open the cover. "We gotta do it," he said.

"All of us? I don't think she'd want us all to read it," I said.

"She would if it means we're going to find her," Sam said.

"You do it," Gus said, and handed the journal back to me. "I don't want to know what goes on in her head. It's probably all about Griffin." He frowned.

I took a deep breath and opened the diary.

October 8.
Turkey with cherry glaze? Or Coca-Cola?
Betty's refusing to eat canned chicken. Maybe I've
spoiled her. Or maybe I've turned her into a gourmand?

October 9.
Idea: butterscotch muffins with peach filling.
Bought a very nice rubber cat stamp at the mall today.
Stamp on menus? Would be pretty. Fern puts her
poodle stamp on everything.

October 10.
Roast chicken with garlic stuffing and sage. Rosemary?
Spoke on the phone with Rosa. Looks like I might go to
L.A. for Christmas. What would I wear there? I know I
won't fit in.

"It's all about food, clothes, and Betty," I said. Then I flipped through to the later passages. "Wait. Here's some more."

November 4.
Betty threw up this morning. Did she eat the poinsettia?
I had a dream about Gus last night. He kissed me in
the gazebo on Main Street. Is there something sensitive
under that gruff exterior? I know there must be. Do I
actually like him? What am I thinking?

"What is it?" Gus asked. "Is it about Griffin?"

"No—um—more food stuff," I said. I looked up at Gus. Would Wilda want him to know what she'd written? I doubted it—I'd cringe with humiliation if Colin knew everything I'd written about him in my journal.

"Flip to the end," Sam said impatiently. "To the last few days. See if she says something that'll give us a clue."

January 2.
Griffin made dinner for us tonight. He's so handsome
and charming and he makes such good chicken. Maybe
I was imagining it, but I think he was flirting with me
tonight. No—I was probably imagining it.

It doesn't matter anyway. It's Gus who has my heart,
even if he's too embarrassed of me to acknowledge it.

January 3.
So much to update! Griffin wants to take me on a trip!
I'll write more tomorrow—

That's where the diary ended.

There was a letter stashed next to the last entry, dated the day before Wilda disappeared:

Wilda, ma chérie,

Ever since we met, I've been awed by your love-liness. You are an unforgettable beauty, unique in all the world, like a rare blue chanterelle or the Château Pétrus I once savored in Pomerol. I am planning to take you on the trip of your dreams. Where and when will be a surprise—

GG

"What is it?" Sam asked. "What does it say?"

"It doesn't really make sense," I said, reading the journal entry again, and then the letter. "She says one thing one day, and the next day it seems like—well—"

I finally showed the journal entries and the letter to them. Gus's nose turned pink as he read her diary, and his face screwed up as he finished Griffin's letter. He handed them to Sam.

"Maybe Griffin didn't write this, or that note before," Sam suggested.

Gus nodded. "We need to get these analyzed. Wilda's last journal entry, too. Someone could've planted these to throw us off track, not expecting that Wilda's missing suitcase would be found."

We took the journal and the note with us, and left Wilda's apartment.

The next morning, Gus and Sam took Griffin's notes and Wilda's journal to a handwriting analyst in Indianapolis, along with the books that Griffin had signed for Mackenzie's mom, for comparison. They also planned to search for Griffin's rental car at the Indianapolis airport and area hotels.

I had to go back to school. Just before second period, Pete came up to me in the hall.

"I want to thank you for helping make my dreams come true," he said.

"What?"

"For helping bring my Conundrum to the masses. I'm thinking after the show I might sell the idea to Taco Bell. My agent says there's been interest."

"Your agent?"

"Nubbs the DP? He told me it's good to have representation, so he gave me a number in L.A."

I couldn't believe this.

"I mean, it's too bad about Wilda and Griffin, though I'm sure they're off somewhere together, very happy. Mrs. Philbert gave me a pass to get out of school after third period this whole week, for the shoot."

He didn't sound too concerned that Wilda and Griffin were missing. I squinted at him. "Hey—what did you do on Sunday night?"

"I saw *Big Night* at Fred's theater—the seven-o'clock showing. Why do you want to know?"

I shrugged. "Just—well, never mind." I wished him good luck with the show and walked to my next class.

I checked with Fred and he confirmed that Pete was at the movie that night. He had an alibi.

"So we can cross him off our suspect list," I told Gus and Sam when I met them in Gus's office after school.

"What did you find out in Indy?" I asked.

"The handwritings were a match," Gus told me. "Wilda wrote all her diary entries herself, and Griffin wrote both those notes. No forgeries." He sounded disappointed.

"It doesn't make sense, though," Sam said. "Say those notes are true and they did run off together—then why would her suitcase have been thrown in the basement?"

None of us had an answer.

"And it still doesn't explain her leaving Betty, and you," I said to Gus.

"There's a lot that doesn't make sense," Gus said, looking depressed. "We did database, public-records, and Internet searches today on all the crew and Griffin, and not much came up." He and Sam had also had no luck finding Griffin's rental car, and no one resembling Wilda and Griffin had checked into the hotels they visited.

"This is weird, though," Sam said. "Remember how Blaine said Griffin was married before? Well, there's no record of it. Though there was a record on Topher. He was arrested once and charged with assault, though not convicted."

"So what's our plan now?" I asked. I didn't want to say it out loud, but most of the facts seemed to be pointing to Wilda and Griffin having run away together.

Gus slumped in his chair and fiddled with his hands. "Maybe I'm crazy, but in my gut I know she didn't take off with that guy," he said. "I know she didn't."

Sam and I nodded. I thought we should listen to what he felt, even if we couldn't prove whether his gut feeling was true yet.

"What next, then?" Sam asked.

"We're going to pay a little visit to Ye Olde Venice Inn, see what we can find." Gus held out a key ring.

"Is that—?" I asked.

Gus nodded. "Thankfully hotel key cards have yet to come to Venice. These are the master keys for the whole inn."

"Where did you get them?" Sam asked.

He smiled proudly. "Let's just say the night clerk likes to drink a lot and is a very sound sleeper. I checked the crew's schedule and they're filming out at Loveland Dairy till seven o'clock. So that gives us three hours."

The phone rang then; Gus picked it up. "Jenkins Agency. Yes, this is he." He grabbed a pen. "Oh, I see. That's right—Griffin Gateaux. I'll be there as soon as I can."

"What happened?" Sam and I asked.

"Griffin's rental car was found in the Bloomington airport long-term parking lot. Someone left it there Sunday night. No one saw who parked it. I'm going to check the car for prints and clues, and see what I find. You two go on to the inn without me."

"Do you think Wilda and Griffin parked it there?" I asked.

He shook his head. "I think someone is taking great pains to try and make it look like they ran off. See what you can dig up at the inn. Time is running out—with each day that passes our chances of finding them drop. We need to hurry. And please—be careful."

Ye Olde Venice Inn was the same motel that Sam and I had stayed in our first night in Venice; we hadn't been back since. It felt strange to go back there now—so much had changed in our lives in the last six months. Back then I had no idea I'd eventually be slipping in the side door and surreptitiously sneaking into people's rooms.

The inn was deserted. There were only ten rooms; Sam nervously jingled the keys as we opened the first one. It turned out to be Nubbs's (we checked the name on his luggage tags). There were local tourist brochures strewn about, and long brown cigarette butts in the ashtray—the kind Yvonne smoked. But no clues. Yvonne's room was next door, and I admired the wealth of high-end cosmetics on every inch of available space: Benefit, Laura Mercier, Hard Candy, Nars, Stila.

"You're staring at that makeup the same way Zayde gazes at the birds through the window," Sam said.

"I know." I sighed, and lovingly examined a Hard Candy Chococicle lip gloss.

It didn't look like she was sleeping there—hers was the only bed we'd seen that was perfectly made. We moved to the next room.

It was Blaine MacPhail's—we could tell by the receipts on the dresser. He had a deluxe room, which in Venice meant that it was about ten feet larger and had an old sofa in it. There were eight pairs of sunglasses on his dresser, a case of Evian, and three Slim-Fast bars. He'd brought his own Thighmaster, and when I opened his closet I groaned.

"Sam. Check this out."

There were three dresses—two black Chanels and one blue-striped Diane von Furstenberg. There were also three large pink nighties.

"What's Blaine doing with all this stuff?" I asked.

"I don't know if we want to know," Sam said. "They look like they're his size." There was also a pair of extremely large pink high heels in the bottom of the closet—the same size as Blaine's other shoes.

"Interesting," I said. "Does this count as a clue?"

Sam hesitated. "I guess. Even if we don't know where it fits in."

The next room was Nikki's. There was a half-empty bottle of red wine on the night table, and stacks of *Gourmet, Saveur, and Bon Appétit* magazines on her dresser; she'd even brought her own bowl of wax fruit to decorate the night table. We searched around through all her things, and at the bottom of a drawer jammed with clothes Sam found this:

Ma chérie Nikkita,

I am in awe of your loveliness. You are an unforgettable beauty, unique in all the world, like the rarest black truffle or the Château de Vosne-Romanée La Romanée I once tasted in Burgundy. Pack a bag. Tomorrow I am taking you to Brugge.

GG

It was dated a month ago. "What, does he have a template for these letters or something? Can't he come up with an original one? What a cheeseball," I said.

"Why did she save it?" Sam asked. "Maybe she still has feelings for him."

"I didn't realize they'd been together that recently," I said, staring at the date again. "Maybe she was jealous of all the attention he was giving to Wilda."

"Jealous enough to do something to him and Wilda?"

"I really hope not."

The next room we entered was Griffin's. We looked around excitedly, certain we'd find something.

It was a mess. We sorted through the piles of his silk pajamas on the floor, boxer shorts with pictures of danc-ing frogs, old copies of French newspapers, and half-eaten tins of Belgian biscuits. It was like an upscale version of Gus's messy apartment. We found his dual French-American passport, which meant they hadn't left the country, I hoped. But after we'd searched for longer than we had in any of the other rooms, nothing helpful came up.

Disheartened, we moved on to Fitz's. I fished a pic-ture of Blaine out of his trash, onto which someone had drawn a Satan-style mustache and goatee. We found an odd selection of comic books, including several titled *Yummy Fur,* but nothing incriminating. In Sniffen's and Bob and Mick's rooms we found lots of girlie magazines, empty beer cans, and boxes of Little Debbie Swiss cake rolls, but that was it.

We had two rooms left. Topher's was filled with tie-dyed T-shirts and Grateful Dead and Phish CDs, and a snapshot of Nikki. I found something else as I rummaged through his sock drawer: something gleaming and silver with an N monogram on the handle.

"Oh my God. Topher has Nikki's knife." I stepped back.

"Don't touch it!" Sam yelled. "It's evidence."

We stared in the drawer, at the knife in a sea of socks.

"Do you think he used it?" Sam asked, looking worried.

"I just hope they're okay," I said. My stomach turned over. "Gus said Topher had that arrest for assault. I wonder—I mean—do you think he could have—?"

"I don't know."

"What should we do?" I asked.

"Gus is on his way to Bloomington." She had our cell phone with her and tried calling him, but there was no answer. "He might be out of range. Look, there's just one more room. Let's go through it, and try Gus again in a few minutes. Then we can figure out what to do."

We unlocked the door to the last room, which was Krista's. It was spotlessly clean, with a silk nightgown hanging on the closet door and plush cashmere slippers by the bed. There were hardly any personal items except for her binder of notes for the show. I leafed through it but there didn't seem to be anything incriminating inside—just scripts and recipes, line notes and accounting invoices for the network. In the back was her passport—also a dual French-American one, like Griffin's. I read through the invoices quickly.

"This is weird—this shows she flew from New York City to Indianapolis on December 26, for one night— that's a week before the crew arrived in Venice. I wonder why she did that."

"It was probably a scouting trip," Sam suggested. "I bet she needed to scout out the location before they awarded the official prize—to make sure it was worthy of a show."

On the night table was a blank pad of hotel notepaper and a pencil.

"Oh, wait—I saw this on *Murder, She Wrote*," I said as I took the Ye Olde Venice Inn pencil and shaded over the top piece of the pad so whatever had been written on it before would come through. I vaguely made out one word: *Chocosub*.

"That's really helpful," Sam said drily. "Sounds like she ordered a chocolate sandwich or something."

The name sounded familiar. It took me half a second to remember. "It's an old candy bar—Colin and Mackenzie told me about it—it used to be big in Indiana ten years ago or something—"

I heard a noise at the door. I looked up.

"*What* are you *doing* here?"

It was Krista. She folded her arms and her eyes bulged at us.

"We—we're. We're—" I stuttered. I felt like I had when I was twelve and got caught shoplifting lipstick in Rite Aid. I thought my heart was going to drop onto the floor.

"*What* are you doing in my *room*?" She glanced

around at all her things, at her dresser and bed and night table.

"It's just—because—you know—" I started to babble.

"This is illegal," Krista said. "Are you stealing something? I'm going to call the police."

Sam regained her composure. "We're investigating the case, and we've discovered something important. We found the missing knife which Nikki said was stolen. It's in Topher's room," Sam said. "We were looking for the culprit and we think we've found him. I'm sorry you found us in your room, too—we were being thorough," she said.

I hoped Krista would be understanding; she seemed shocked at the information. "Topher stole the knife?" she asked. Her eyes bulged even more.

"We just hope he hasn't used it. He's in love with Nikki and was jealous of Griffin, we think. We need to tell Gus we found it so we can get it analyzed and turn Topher in to the police," I said.

She put her hand to her head. "Topher...oh my God. Do you know—I saw him get in his car Sunday night, around the time Wilda and Griffin disappeared. I didn't think anything of it then, but..."

"You did? He told Gus he went for a walk," I said.

Krista bit her lip. "Then he lied to you." She reached in her pocket and pulled out her car keys. "I think I know where he might have gone that night. I heard him telling Nikki about this place he knew of that's twenty minutes away, this abandoned building—maybe we can go there, if it's not too late. Maybe—there's a chance—that's where Wilda and Griffin could be."

"Do you know where it is?" Sam asked.

She nodded. "I'm pretty sure."

We followed her out to her car. I hoped she was right—that we might find Wilda and Griffin there, and I prayed we weren't too late.

We drove past snow-covered fields and meadows through the middle of nowhere for at least twenty minutes until I saw a building in the distance that looked like a huge brown bubble parked in a field. As we approached it I could read the letters on the side: CHOCOSUB.

"This is where you think they are?" I asked.

She stopped the car, reached into her purse, and pulled out something pink and feathery, like a miniboa or a little purse.

I looked closer. It wasn't a feather boa or a purse.

It was the missing gun.

Ten

Krista told us to walk toward the door of the factory. "Griffin has a regular pattern—arrives in a new town and within two hours he's found a new bimbo to fall for. He sends her a love note, they run off together—same old story. When we were married he was doing the same thing, behind my back. Then he started telling me about it, as if I couldn't wait to hear all the details. This time, he told me he was falling for Wilda almost as soon as he met her."

We backed away from her toward the factory, and tried to sound calm.

"You were married to Griffin?" Sam asked. I wondered if Sam was thinking of the *Oprah* episode we'd once watched together. *Talk to the crazy person,* the cop on the show had advised. *Remain calm. Avoid making sudden moves.*

"In France. That's where we met. He was a nobody. I discovered him, I gave him his first job, I made him who he was. And now I'm taking it all back."

"Where are they?" Sam asked.

She waved toward the factory. "In there. That's where I left them three days ago. They're probably dehydrated beyond belief and hypothermic by now, if they're still alive. Humans can only live three days without water, isn't that right?"

"But what about Wilda? Why include her in this—it's not her fault," Sam said.

"I couldn't make it seem like Griffin had run off without having a woman for him to run off with, could I?" Krista asked. "I'm sorry you got swept into this, too. I didn't plan it this way. I wanted Griffin to suffer slowly and painfully the way I have. Watching him woo one woman after another after another...as if the world is one big plate and the women are hors d'oeuvres for him to eat...well, I hope he's dying a long suffering death in there. I'm sorry you became involved in it, too...but if you found something in my room, you could've told someone and ruined everything."

The feathers Yvonne had glued to the gun flapped in the wind. *It's fake*, I reminded myself. *Yvonne told us she thought the gun was fake.*

I'd never have imagined how scary a middle-aged lady waving a wad of pink feathers could be, but Sam and I were terrified. And even if there was only a tiny chance that the gun was real, we definitely didn't want to find out the hard way.

She herded us toward the factory door, took out a key, and unlocked the bolt. It was quiet inside. Then she pushed us in and locked the door behind us.

I blinked in the darkness; I couldn't see anything until my eyes adjusted. We heard the engine start and Krista's car drive off.

"Sophie? Sam? Is that you?" Wilda's voice came out

of the dark, and before I knew it, she'd engulfed us in a huge hug. When my eyesight adjusted, I saw her and Griffin, huge hulking metal machines, and candy wrappers in a pile on the floor. I looked around the room. It was modeled to appear like the inside of a submarine; there was just a thin row of circular windows over ten feet above us.

"Is she—is Krista gone?" Griffin whimpered. He limped toward us. "We were afraid she'd find out we were still alive and try to finish us off."

"I'm so glad you're okay," Sam said. "She told us you'd be dehydrated by now..."

Griffin and Wilda exchanged glances. "We would have been, but we found this." Wilda led us to another room down a long dark corridor, which housed huge boxes and fifty-five-gallon drums. One box was filled with Chocosub bars.

"Krista didn't know the factory's stockroom still contains a huge stash of Chocosubs. They're filled with so many preservatives, they last forever!" she said. "There's soda water here also, and we lived off the candy bars until we found another stash of canned ingredients. Griffin made the best dishes out of condensed milk, sugar, nuts, and nougat." She pointed down another corridor. "There's a test kitchen with a gas stove over there. Griffin fiddled with it and got the gas valve working—thank God there's still a connection—and we lit the stove with his lighter. We keep the stove turned on for warmth, too. We wouldn't have survived without it."

"How did you get here? What happened?" Sam asked.

"Sunday night after the filming had wrapped, Krista told us she wanted to check out the Chocosub factory, to scout it out for filming—the show often does little bits on quirky places, you know. She didn't tell anyone but us about taking us here. After we wrapped filming in the diner, she said she had something to fetch back in her room, so she drove to the hotel with Blaine and then met us back at the diner later. We drove here, and then she locked us inside," Wilda said. "It took us a few minutes to realize what had happened. And that there's no way out."

"No way out?" My voice wavered.

"Well—hopefully we can find one," she said. "With your help."

"Is the gun Krista stole from props real?" Sam asked Griffin. She described it to him.

Griffin shook his head. "That's a water gun."

"Oh no." We'd just gotten forced into an abandoned factory with a water gun. I moaned.

"It's all my fault," Griffin said. "I'm so sorry you got involved in this." He sat down on the floor and started gently weeping.

"Let him cry," Wilda said. "He's been doing this a lot. He needs the release." She sighed.

"So he was married to Krista?" Sam asked Wilda, trying to make sense of everything that had just happened.

"Fifteen years ago, when they lived in France. They were divorced there, too."

"If it happened in France I guess that's why it didn't come up on our public-records search," Sam said.

"But Griffin left that note about you running away," I said. We told her about the note left in the diner.

Griffin took a deep breath. "I wrote that note and signed it from both of us because I assumed that of course Wilda would come with me. I was wrong," he said. "Wilda knows better. She's too good for the likes of me." He sniffled.

"He's been telling me about all the women he's known," Wilda whispered. "Woo-hoo, there's a lot of them." She smiled. "He was going to try to convince me to leave town with him late that night. I told him while we were driving with Krista that I didn't want to go. I guess she took that note and pinned it to the tablecloth later. It fit in with her plan."

"And she must have hid your suitcase, too." We told her how Betty had found it in the basement.

"Oh, my Betty!" Wilda said, shaking her head. "I had catnip in that suitcase—I'd brought it back for her from L.A."

And I'd thought Betty was just a good detective.

"Now we just have to figure how to get out of here," Sam said. Her eyes brightened for a moment and she pulled the cell phone out of her jacket pocket. She blinked at it. "No service." Her voice cracked.

A part of me wanted to scream with fear—how would anyone ever find us in here? How long could we live off Chocosubs and weird nougat creations? I tried to remain calm and cool and collected. I thought: *WWSHD:*

What would Sherlock Holmes do? Or maybe WWNDD was more fitting for this situation. What *would* Nancy Drew do? She was always getting locked in places.

I stared up at the row of portholelike windows above us. Whose dumb idea was it to make a factory look like a submarine?

Sam was eyeing the windows, too. "Do those windows open? I wonder if Sophie could fit through," she said.

"They do. Griffin and I tried that—I stood on his shoulders and I just reached the window, but I couldn't fit my hips through. And then when I came down Griffin lost his balance and hurt his ankle."

Griffin nodded. His tears had subsided and he put his head in his hands.

"Can you try lifting Sophie up?" Sam asked him.

He shook his head and rubbed his ankle. "It's still killing me. I can barely stand up on it."

"Just you or I plus Sophie won't be tall enough to reach that window," Sam said to Wilda. "We'll need all three of us."

"A human ladder? Like in the circus?" I asked. "With me on top?"

Sam nodded.

"Oh God," I said. "I'm gonna die."

Sam climbed onto Wilda's shoulders, and it took me about fifteen tries to get up onto Sam's. Then Wilda slowly made her way toward the window. We swayed like a set of bad clowns, and fell over onto the sea of bubble wrap that we'd arranged from the materials in the factory to prevent us from breaking any bones. Finally, after popping a hundred bubble-wrap bubbles, bruising both my legs, and falling a dozen more times, we reached the window.

"This isn't what I meant when I said I wanted to join the circus as a kid," I told Sam.

"What? I can't hear you—you're squishing my ear," she shouted.

I reached up and opened the window, then grabbed the edge and pushed my shoulders through it. They fit. Sam helped hold my feet, and I squeezed my middle through.

"Keep pushing! Keep going!" Sam, Wilda, and Griffin shouted below me. "Run like crazy when you get out! Look for houses down the road! Don't forget how to get back here!"

There was a drop below the window, but thankfully several feet of snow had drifted up to the side of the factory. I finally squeezed my butt through the window, and dove out. I slid down the snowy slope below like a human sled. Unfortunately one sneaker had fallen off into the factory as I pushed myself through the window. I gazed up at the window and heard a thumping noise. A few minutes later, my sneaker came flying out. A distant cheer rose up from the factory. My sock was soaking wet but I tied the sneaker on. And then I ran.

I ran faster than I ever had in my life. I ran for miles— I didn't know how many. I just kept going down the road until I finally saw a light. It was a farmhouse. I ran up the front porch and knocked on the door.

A woman in a blue cardigan opened it. She looked startled to see me, sweaty and out of breath, my skin bright red from the cold.

"I have an emergency—I need to use your phone. Can I please make a call?"

I made two calls: to Gus and Colin. They arrived together and picked me up at the farmhouse, and we drove to the factory.

Colin brought a huge down comforter and wrapped me in it; I collapsed in his arms and told them everything that had happened. Gus called Chief Callowe as we sped to the factory and relayed the information to him. Callowe said he'd get a warrant for Krista's arrest right away.

I'd told Colin to bring whatever tools he had to get the bolt open, and he did. It took several tries, but it came off the door. In the end, that hammer I'd given him turned out to be a good present after all.

When we opened the Chocosub door, Sam and Wilda and Griffin rushed out. I hugged my sister tighter than I ever had before.

Then Gus did something completely uncharacteristic: he kissed Wilda on the lips in front of everyone.

By the time we reached home, Krista had already been arrested.

The rest of the crew was waiting for us in the diner. "You should've seen her," Nubbs said. "'I'm getting my lawyer to whop you with a wrongful imprisonment suit, blah blah blah,'" he imitated in a squeaky voice.

Gus asked more questions of the crew, to make sense of everything.

"Topher did take the knife from Nikki's tool set—he liked it because it had Nikki's monogram, he says. A bit odd, but apparently true. He didn't use it for anything," Gus told us.

"And I bet Krista came out here the week before the shoot to check out the Chocosub factory—she was probably devising a way to lock Griffin up even then," Sam said.

A doctor examined Wilda and Griffin, and tended to Griffin's sprained ankle. Aside from suffering from too much sugar and a great deal of stress, he pronounced them to be all right.

After Wilda and Griffin finished explaining their ordeal in full detail to the crew, Blaine actually looked excited. "This is just what we need for the ratings—a survival cooking show, using some of the recipes you created in the factory," Blaine said. "Nix the burrito boy! God, did that suck."

Eleven

"Welcome to *Griffin on the Go*! I'm your host, Griffin Gateaux, and we have a special edition of the show for you tonight. It will be in two parts. First is the winner of our Best American Recipe contest—Wilda Higgins's Petal Diner dumpling soup from the lovely town of Venice, Indiana. In the second half of the show we'll be featuring two special recipes I developed, for survival brittle and survival soda, during a recent adventure, as well as a few important tips you might need to know if you're ever in a life-threatening situation."

Sam, Colin, Gus, Mackenzie, and Fred and I sat in the back during the taping. "What kind of tips is he going to have?" Colin whispered to me. "Bring candy?"

"Now let me introduce the beautiful, indomitable Wilda Higgins, owner of the Petal Diner, where we're broadcasting from today."

Wilda smiled at the camera. "Before we get started, I want to thank two very dear friends of mine—this recipe originated from one of their mother's delicious creations. I changed some elements of it, but the credit goes to them. Thank you, girls. These dumplings are for you."

Sam and I smiled.

Griffin pointed to a pile of ground Ritz cracker crumbs and a plate of chicken. "The most interesting thing to note about these dumplings is the hybrid of ingredients—they bear a resemblance to the traditional European dumpling, the American cracker, and the Jewish matzo ball. But they also have their own unique identity."

Sam and I exchanged looks. Hopefully no one would remember the Jewish matzo-ball reference.

Betty hopped onto the counter and started nibbling the plate of chicken.

"CUT!" Blaine yelled. "GET THAT CAT OFF THE SET!"

"My perfect plate of chicken," Nikki moaned, and rushed to the counter.

"Cut, cut, cut," Blaine grumbled. "From the top."

"That man has two really nice Chanel dresses hanging in his closet," I whispered to Mackenzie. "Griffin caught him wearing one of the show's wardrobe dresses once, years ago. That's why Blaine could never fire Griffin for all his disappearances from the set—he knew too much."

She nodded. "I bet he looks good in Chanel."

Nikki rearranged the plate of chicken; Blaine ordered the cameras to roll, and Griffin and Wilda repeated their lines.

"The word *dumpling* can refer to any type of boiled or steamed dough—or it can be a term of affection," Griffin said.

"Please don't call Wilda your dumpling," Sam whispered.

"She's my dumpling," Gus said matter-of-factly.

"You're my dumpling," Fred said to Mackenzie. She laughed.

"You're *my* dumpling," Colin said to me.

"Guys. Ick," Sam said. "You're grossing me out here."

"QUIET ON THE SET!" Blaine shouted at us.

Out of the corner of my eye I saw Alby sitting in the corner by himself, watching the taping. I didn't know if I was imagining it or not, but I thought he was staring at Sam and me.

"Why's he looking at us like that?" I asked my sister.

She shrugged. "Just forget about him."

The Petal Diner finally reopened for regular business the morning after the show finished taping and the crew had left town. Sam, Josh, and Colin and I walked there for breakfast.

"Finally things can get back to normal," I said.

As we approached the diner we saw Wilda standing outside. Her hands were shoved in the pockets of her apron and she paced around in a little circle, looking frustrated.

"What's going on?" Sam asked her.

"The weirdest woman is in there right now," Wilda said. "I just needed to get some fresh air—this woman, a tall skinny lady from New York City, is meeting with Officer Alby, and she's driving me crazy. In addition to asking for Sweet'N Low five times, which I don't have, and asking the calorie count of every item on the menu, she haggled about the prices. She was so rude..." Wilda sighed. "I better get back in there, though. Wish me luck."

Wilda went inside the diner, and Sam and I exchanged looks. I peeked in the window and my heart stopped.

"*Enid*," I breathed. She was sitting exactly where Hertznick had sat with Alby before Christmas.

Sam and I ducked below the windows just as we had then.

Josh, who knew who Enid was, looked panicked; Colin looked completely confused.

"You need to go hide, right now," Josh said.

"What's going on?" Colin asked.

"Can they hide out at your place?" Josh asked.

"Of course—sure," Colin said. "What—why?"

"I'll see what we can do to distract her and keep her away from you. Wait for us at Colin's in the meantime," Josh said. "Now go!"

We started running. We reached Colin's shop and I got the key from under the goose.

"Josh will explain it to him," I told Sam. "Right? And Colin will stick up for us?"

"I'm sure he will," Sam said. Her face had gone white. We were panting as we locked the door behind us. When we finally caught our breath, Sam started pacing.

"What's she doing here in Venice?"

"I have no idea." Sam ran her hands through her hair. "I can't believe this."

It felt like we were waiting in Colin's apartment for hours for Josh and Colin to return, though it was only twenty minutes later that they knocked on the door.

Colin stared at me. "Josh told me everything," he said. He gave me a hug, but it was sort of awkward; he looked confused and overwhelmed.

"How did Enid get here? How did she end up talking to Alby?" Sam asked.

"Apparently Alby had the first smart idea of his life: when he heard the Jewish matzo ball mentioned, he called Hertznick. Hertznick told Alby Enid had fired him, but gave Alby Enid's number," Josh explained.

"Alby's had such a vendetta against you since you turned him in for the pet case—I guess calling Enid was his revenge," Colin said. It was weird to hear the name Enid come out of Colin's mouth.

"Did they leave the diner? Where'd they go?" I asked.

"Alby was taking Enid to walk by your house, and then to Gus's office next," Josh said.

"Oh God—what if Gus tells her the truth?" I asked.

"We need to warn him," Sam said.

"We can warn him—it's not safe for you to go there," Josh said.

Sam shook her head. "No—I need to tell him myself. Or he might slip—he needs to know the whole story, he can't be surprised at all...if he slips up, then it's all over."

"Enid and Alby were walking—if we drive to Gus's office right now, we might be able to cut them off," Josh said.

We climbed into Colin's van, ducked down, and drove

to Gus's office. Enid and Alby weren't there yet. "We'll guard outside, and if we see them, we'll warn you," Josh said.

"How?" Sam asked.

"We'll honk the horn three times," Colin said.

Sam and I ran up the stairs to Gus's office. We burst in the door; he was sitting at his desk, playing solitaire on the computer.

"We need to tell you something," Sam said. "We've never told you this before, but it's really important and I hope you'll forgive us...but a woman named Enid is on her way over here right now, and she's our—"

"Stepmother," Gus said.

Our mouths opened.

A car horn honked three times; Enid and Alby were approaching.

"How—?" I started to ask, but Gus led us into the hall and opened the door next to his office, where there was a bathroom with three stalls. "Get in there," he said. "And stay there till I say it's safe to come out. And don't worry. I can handle Enid."

So Gus knew. How did Gus know? Sam and I didn't dare speak; the walls were thin between the bathroom and his office.

Through the bathroom wall, we heard the door to his office open. My heart plummeted.

"Gus, we have something very important to discuss with you. This lady here, Miss Gutmyre, has come all the way from New York City to talk to you."

"What is it, Alby?" Gus barked.

"We think your assistants, Sam and Sophie, are two missing, runaway Jewish girls who stole Miss Gutmyre's money," Alby said. He introduced Enid.

"Hello," Enid said. I shivered at hearing her voice. "I hope you haven't had the misfortune of meeting them—they're miserable girls. Criminals. I have a picture of them here. They're not pretty, either."

I tried not to yelp in protest.

"These girls look nothing like the two who work for me. You two are wasting my time here," Gus said.

"You know that if you're lying, you could lose your PI license and go to jail," Alby said.

"What are you talking about, Alby? Is this because of your pet-thief ring? You still sulky about that? We never pressed charges..."

"Pet-thief ring?" Enid asked.

"Some, um, unruly animals around town," Alby mumbled.

"I hate animals," Enid said.

"Just look at these photos carefully, Gus," Alby said. "They're a little old, but imagine these girls a few years later. These are definitely the same sisters."

I heard papers rustling. "Please. My assistants are Christian, from Cleveland, named Sam and Fiona, and I'll stand up for them till the day I die."

"And when did you first meet them? July, right? That's when they left New York City," Alby said in his squeaky voice.

"As a matter of fact, I first met the girls in June. They

were looking to settle in a different town first. I knew
their parents through friends, and decided I'd help them
settle here."

I couldn't believe Gus was lying for us.

"The girls were with me in June," Enid muttered. "Did
you make me come all the way here for nothing?" she
snapped at Alby. "That ticket is nonrefundable. I spent
two hundred and fifty dollars on it."

"I'm certain they're the same—"

"I'm a detective who specializes in missing persons.
Do you think I'd hire two missing persons to work for
me?" Gus asked. He chuckled.

"You specialize in missing persons?" Enid asked him.
"What do you charge to take on a case?"

"Ten thousand per person," Gus said.

"Forget it," Enid muttered.

We heard the door to his office creak open.

"Officer Alby, Miss Gutmyre, if you don't mind, I have
some serious work to do," Gus said.

Gus had lied for us. Sam and I stared at each other.
She squeezed my hand. From his calm manner of speaking, it sounded like he had probably known the truth
about us for a long time.

"I'm sorry, Miss Gutmyre," Alby said in the hall,
sounding defeated.

"You lured me to this godforsaken town, made me
spend money on the flight, that god-awful breakfast this
morning...of course those girls aren't here—what New
Yorker could spend more than a few hours in this
place?" Enid complained. "At least you can drive me to

the airport so I don't have to pay for a shuttle. Wait. I need to use the bathroom."

I stopped breathing. Sam and I clamored inside a stall and locked the door. I crouched on the back of the toilet while Sam sat there with her feet on the floor, trying to act natural.

"Two hundred and fifty dollars—what a waste," Enid muttered as she opened the stall door next to ours and went to the bathroom. "And I ate too much again. That omelet must have been five hundred calories. The strawberry was three. The tea had real sugar in it, let's say twenty calories...that leaves me seven hundred calories for lunch and dinner..."

The same old Enid. She flushed, and then she left.

After ten minutes, Gus opened the bathroom door. "They drove off. She's gone," he said.

"Thank you," Sam said quietly.

"Thank you, Gus," I said. I hugged him.

"You don't need to thank me."

"How long have you known?" Sam asked.

He stared up at the ceiling. "I guess I figured it out about six months ago."

"That's when we moved here," Sam said.

"I know. I'm a pretty good detective."

Sam and I smiled.

He shook his head. "Enid Gutmyre, what a piece of work." And that was the last he mentioned of her.

I didn't know how to handle the fact that Colin knew who we were now. What would I say to him? *So I'm re-*

ally a whole different person from who you thought I was, ha ha ha! Oops—forgot to mention that I was someone else!

On New Year's Eve I'd said to myself that I loved him, but what did he feel? I didn't even know if he loved Sophie Scott; who knows what he felt toward Sophie Shattenberg. Maybe we'd have to start all over again from scratch. Back to just being friends.

Josh was waiting for us on our porch. "Colin and I followed Alby and Enid to the outskirts of town when they left Gus's building, to make sure they were leaving," he said. "They're definitely gone. So everything went okay with Gus?" he asked us.

Sam nodded. "Thanks so much for helping us—I don't know what we would've done if you hadn't." She gave Josh a hug.

"How did Colin take it when you told him the truth?" I asked Josh.

"He was definitely overwhelmed, but he's such a good guy—he understands. I didn't tell him the whole story; you need to explain the details to him. He wanted to be alone for a while—he's at his shop waiting for you. You should go over there."

"I will." I went up to my room first, and took out a package that had just come in the mail the day before. It was a book I'd ordered for him over the Internet—a rare, early edition of the poems of Edna St. Vincent Millay. It included "Women Have Loved Before as I Love Now," which was the poem I'd been reading the day I first met Colin in his shop.

I wrapped it up and put it in my knapsack. I walked over to his shop.

Colin looked nervous when he opened the door. I wondered what was going through his head—would he forgive me for not having told him the truth months ago?

He had set out two sandwiches on the table. "I was hoping you'd stop by—I picked these up from Wilda for you—we never got a chance to eat this morning, with everything that happened."

"I know—I'm starving."

We ate our sandwiches, and afterward I said, "So...I guess I should explain things in detail." I paused. "Our parents didn't die in a car accident. My mom died in a carjacking in Indianapolis six and a half years ago. My dad died in New York City, in Queens, in July." I took a deep breath and told him the whole story, about Enid, the money, our fleeing, and our car breaking down. I didn't leave anything out.

He listened to all of it, nodding, absorbing. After I finished he said, "Do you want to play a game of Lorna Scrabble?"

"Oh...okay..." It wasn't exactly the response I'd expected. Hadn't he heard anything I'd just said? Was this his way of trying to make things seems normal, or something? Maybe he needed to ignore the new information until he could get used to it.

He went to get the Scrabble set. The photo album Sam and I'd found the last time we hid in his shop was sitting on the coffee table. I opened it. I stared at the photos of his dad and mom, and of Colin as a kid. His mom was so pretty. I gazed at her picture. What had she been like? I wondered if she and my parents were some-where together—I pictured them up in some big rocking chair in the sky—or Colin's mom and my mom together at some ethereal beauty parlor, gossiping about us. I smiled, thinking about it.

Colin appeared beside me with the Scrabble set. "Oh—I was going to show those pictures to you."

"I saw them once before, actually." I told him how we'd hid out in his shop during Hertznick's trip to Venice—I figured I might as well come clean about everything. I hoped he wouldn't mind—and he didn't.

"I wish you could have met her," he said as he looked at his mom's picture.

"I know. I wish I could have, too."

"I wish I could have met your parents," he said.

"You would've liked them," I said. I knew my parents would've loved Colin. Maybe, wherever they were, they knew all about him. I hoped so.

He set up the Scrabble set. "Do you want to make some hot chocolate? The mugs are over there."

"Sure." I stood up and went to the sink. I microwaved two mugs of water, opened two instant packets and stirred the mix in, and brought them to the coffee table.

He shifted on the couch. "I took my turn already," he said. "I hope you don't mind."

"Sure, whatever. What's the definit—"

I froze in place. I stared at the Scrabble board. The letters had been arranged in a row:

I L O V E Y O U

"The Lorna Scrabble definition is when you care about someone so much that it doesn't matter what their real name is, or where they're from, or what their story is—it just means that you love them. I've loved you since that first day you walked into my shop. And I still love you, whether you're Sophie Shattenberg or Fiona Scott or from Queens or Cleveland or Timbuktu. I don't care. I love you."

"I—I—I—" I didn't know what to say. Then I just said how I really felt: "I love you, too." Apparently it was plenty, because he kissed me more tenderly than he ever had before.

"I have something for you," I said. I got up and got the gift out of my knapsack. "It's, um, a replacement for the hammer."

"I love the hammer. It came in handy."

"I know, but...well, then consider this a belated extra Chanukah gift." I smiled—I could actually say that to him now.

He unwrapped the Millay book. "This is what you were reading the day we met," he said.

"I know. You quoted the poem 'Women Have Loved Before as I Love Now.'"

"They have?" He smiled.

I nodded. "Very much so," I said, and kissed him.

We kissed on the couch and accidentally knocked the Scrabble letters off the board with our feet. We didn't even stop kissing to pick them up.

The night Wilda's episode of *Griffin on the Go* was going to be broadcast, Colin and I walked to the Petal

Diner to see it. We joined Josh and Sam in a booth.

Wilda had made Petal dumpling soup, survival brittle, and survival soda for everyone. It was the first time I'd actually tasted the dumplings—Sam and I had shied away during the filming.

"These are actually really good," I said as I took another bite.

"I can't believe this is the first time you're trying them," Colin said.

"They are tasty," Josh said. "If not entirely holiday appropriate," he added under his breath.

Gus had an extra-huge portion of all the food.

"He's not exactly kissing me all over town yet, but he held my hand all the way down Main Street yesterday," Wilda told us. She lowered her voice. "We're talking about, well—we might move in together."

"Really? Where? Above the diner?" I asked.

"No. I inherited some property many years back. My parents used to own this big old place, a stone house on the outskirts of town, with a great view of Venice. After they died, I never wanted to live in it. I opened the diner and just wanted to stay here. But we're thinking of fixing it up and moving back in there sometime." She laughed. "No time soon—it'll be a while till we can get that place up and running. But it's fun to dream about it."

"Is it the overlook house?" Sam asked. She described where it was, and Wilda nodded.

"You know about make-out overlook?" I asked Sam when Wilda had walked away. My eyes widened.

"Make-out overlook?" Sam said.

"Um—Colin told me about it," Josh explained sheepishly. "I took Sam there a few times."

I gaped at my sister.

"We just hung out there and—talked," Sam said with a big smile.

"Talked. Just like the chickens do," I said, and we laughed.

Henry, who was sitting at the counter, shushed us. "The show's starting!" he said. Everyone quieted down.

"Welcome to Griffin on the Go*! I'm your host…"*

Wilda had a great screen presence and the shots of Venice were beautiful. It was funny to see the local sights, the cornfields, the meadows, and the canal, with the computer-animated tiny stream of water that Blaine had ordered put into it.

"I wonder if Krista's watching from prison," Wilda said. "Griffin got a pretty high-powered lawyer, so she won't be getting out anytime soon."

"Are you and Griffin still in touch?" I asked Wilda.

"He sent me a postcard from Nantucket. He's filming a piece on fried clams and chowder."

"And no doubt fleeing in a dinghy with a buxom young clam digger," Sam said.

The show ended with Griffin's trademark line: *"Until next week, this is Griffin Gateaux—on the go!"* He trotted off jauntily into the Indiana landscape.

Everyone clapped.

Sam, Josh, and Colin and I raised our glasses of survival soda.

"To Venice," Sam and I said. "The exciting, crazy town that we love."

We toasted.

"And to the people we love," Josh said, staring at Sam.

"To the people we love," I repeated, staring at Colin, and our glasses clinked.

Acknowledgments

Thank you to Jackie Rabb, Dika Lam, and the Reid family, and a special thanks to Sara Shandler and her mother, Nina Shandler, whose buttery matzo ball was the inspiration for this book.